She was not going to die out here.

She told herself that even as a clawlike hand grabbed her hair, rendering her immobile.

She couldn't scream, couldn't move. Terror embedded itself deep in her muscles. She could feel herself shutting down and the world going black as ten-year-old memories crashed in from all sides.

Help me.

As if someone heard her plea, lights shone through the broken window. A car was coming down the hill.

Her assailant pulled her close and whispered harsh words before he took off.

She drew what felt like her first breath when she felt Zach's arms surround her and lift her off the floor.

"It's going to be all right, Elizabeth. I'm here." He pulled her close to his chest.

Even as she burrowed into the comfort of his arms, she recalled the departing words of her assailant and knew they were true. *You will never feel safe again.*

Ever since she found the Nancy Drew books with the pink covers in her country school library, **Sharon Dunn** has loved mystery and suspense. Most of her books take place in Montana, where she lives with three nearly grown children and a spastic border collie. She lost her beloved husband of twenty-seven years to cancer in 2014. When she isn't writing, she loves to hike surrounded by God's beauty.

Books by Sharon Dunn

Love Inspired Suspense

FATAL VENDETTA

SHARON DUNN

HARLEQUIN® LOVE INSPIRED® SUSPENSE

LOVE INSPIRED BOOKS

Recycling programs for this product may not exist in your area.

ISBN-13: 978-0-373-67769-6

Fatal Vendetta

When justice is done it brings joy to the righteous,
but terror to evildoers.
–Proverbs 21:15

For Richard, my friend and soul mate, for bringing me back to the land of the living and teaching me to breathe again.

ONE

Elizabeth Kramer's heartbeat skipped into double time as the fire trucks sped around her KBLK news van. She didn't like the idea that another tragedy had struck Badger, Montana, but knowing that she might make a difference through her news reporting created a sense of excitement in her.

"The police scanner was a good investment." Elizabeth looked over at her cameraman, Dale, who sat behind the wheel.

"Good thing you had it on." Dale kept his eyes focused on the flashing lights of the fire trucks as he pulled back out into traffic. "We should be the first news team there."

The prospect gave her spirits a jolt. Since the move ten years ago back to Montana to rebuild her life and then take care of her dying father, she was determined to succeed as a reporter, to put the past behind her.

When they arrived at the warehouse, flames

shot out of the upper story. Cool summer evening air surrounded Elizabeth as she exited the van. She caught sight of the gathering crowd. Even at a distance, she could see the expressions of shock and fear on the faces of the onlookers. A reminder of why she had chosen to become a reporter in the first place. Her father had been a police officer. To him, work had been about sacrifice and service. Now that he was gone, she wanted to live by his example, using her chosen vocation, the gifts God had given her, as a way to help others.

Elizabeth tugged at the hem of the blazer she'd hurriedly thrown on over her T-shirt and sweats. Dale would shoot her from the waist up. No one would see her cartoon-emblazoned pants.

Her heart raced as she scanned the crowd, recognizing the fire chief and the arson investigator from Badger PD. Interesting. Maybe the fire wasn't an accident. "Let's get some coverage from the eyewitnesses until the first responders can give us some info." She turned a half circle, reading the faces of thirty or so people who had gathered to watch the warehouse burn. Most of them were probably Johnny-come-latelies who would have nothing to contribute about what had happened, but surely somewhere in the crowd was the man or woman who had been here for the early stages of the fire and made the 911 call.

A woman with her arm around a teenage boy offered a welcoming expression. Elizabeth stepped toward her but stopped short when Zachery Beck emerged from the shadows holding a tablet computer. He closed in on the woman before Elizabeth could reach her.

Dale came up behind Elizabeth. He shook his bald head. "How did Zach Beck get here so fast?"

Elizabeth clenched her jaw. "Beats me." She studied the tall, unassuming man. His blond hair was a little too long and wild to qualify for the messy-on-purpose look. The five o'clock shadow and ripped jeans indicated he was a man who didn't care how he looked. He didn't have to care. Zach wrote an independent news blog called *Minute by Minute* that was taking a lot of KBLK's viewer and online base. Zach had a gift for being the first reporter at every major news event. She had to admire his talent even if he did scoop her.

How had he managed to get out in front of her this time?

She moved in closer to listen to Zach question the woman. He was typing as she talked. Did he actually send raw, unedited stories straight to the blog? She'd read his news stories. The articles were polished and professional.

"And when did you first notice the flames shooting out of the upper floors?" Zach offered Elizabeth a nod before turning his attention back to the woman.

The woman drew her son into a tighter hug. Embarrassed, the teenager rolled his eyes, but didn't angle out of his mother's embrace. "We just finished eating at the fried chicken place down the street and we were headed back to our apartment on Wilson Avenue."

Zach asked one detailed question after another. She understood how he managed to get such good interviews. His voice was soft, inviting conversation rather than intimidating. He leaned in anytime the woman spoke. Everything about his body language indicated that the spotlight was on the woman, not him. Was it an act he'd perfected as part of his skill set as a reporter or was he really that humble?

When Zach finished, Elizabeth stepped toward the woman. "Hi, Elizabeth Kramer from KBLK. I wonder if we could get you on camera answering a few questions for us?"

"I already told that man everything I know. It's been a long night for David and me." She turned and walked away, still not letting go of her son.

Elizabeth let out a heavy breath.

Dale came up behind her. "I got some visuals of the fire. We need some talking heads before you do your stand-up."

Fuming over losing the important interview, Elizabeth glanced at the fire chief, who was still engaged with the arson investigator. She walked over to Zach while he filmed the fire.

"Congrats on getting that interview with the eyewitness," Elizabeth said.

Zach offered her a crooked grin. "Yeah, sorry about scooping you on that. Guess I wore her out. She didn't want to be on TV with the beauty queen."

She didn't like it when people brought up her pageant days. That was over a decade ago when she lived in Seattle before her life had fallen apart. How did he even find that out? Had he been investigating her? She swept away the pain that talking about her past produced.

Focus on the story, Elizabeth.

"If you don't mind, I listened to you interview her. I'd like to use some of that info in my report even if I can't get her on camera."

Zach's eyebrow went up. "You do whatever you need to do, Betsy." Then he smiled in a disarming way. His blue eyes had a Paul Newman coolness to them.

She bit her tongue. He knew what her name

was. The jabbing at her happened every time they were both chasing the same story. *Let it go. He's just trying to bait you.* She peered over his shoulder. "Looks like the fire chief and the arson investigator are free."

"I already talked to them. No question about it. The fire was started on purpose, really basic incendiary device."

Elizabeth could not push down her frustration anymore. "How could you possibly have found that out so fast?"

Zach laughed, putting on his best New York accent. "Youse gotta have your sources, lady." He ambled away toward the circle of firefighters, who slapped him on the back. He'd cultivated his relationship with the first responders way more than she had been able to even though her father had been sheriff in a town not too far from Badger.

Elizabeth shook her head. Zach delighted a little too much in their friendly competition. It seemed clear that the humble guy who did the interviews was the act and the always-looking-for-the-upper-hand Zach was the real deal. Too bad. Those blue eyes suggested a much gentler man.

Another news truck pulled into the lot.

Dale leaned close to her. "So what now?"

They would end up getting the same footage as the other station when the police chief made his statement. Since Zachery Beck had stolen her thunder by getting the eyewitness report, she had to find an angle no one else had.

She peered at the faces in the crowd. Sometimes the arsonist showed up to watch the reaction to his work. A large man in a pulled-down baseball hat toward the back of the crowd raised and lowered his head. He'd looked at her only for an instant, but she thought she'd caught a flash of some emotion.

She edged toward him.

The man took a step back, turned and walked away. The darkness behind the warehouse enveloped him. Had she caught a look of guilt on his face, or was she just so desperate for a story angle, she was jumping to conclusions? Maybe he was involved, or it could be that the guy knew something but was afraid to talk. She couldn't call herself a real reporter if she didn't pursue a lead, even a tentative one. She glanced around for Dale, who was filming the firemen working. No time to catch his attention.

Feeling a mixture of fear and excitement, she slipped away from the crowd toward the darkness where the man in the baseball hat had disappeared.

Zachery glanced around. Where had Elizabeth gone? He'd seen her doing her broadcast only a moment ago. She was a good reporter. Way better on camera than he'd ever been. He might be good at finding the stories, but she was great at delivering them.

He watched her every night. Not that he would tell her that, though. He kind of enjoyed their friendly professional jousting. He couldn't believe he'd let it slip he knew about her beauty queen days. It wasn't on the official profile the TV station posted on their website—he'd had to go digging for the information. Wanting to find out more about her was only partially motivated by the know-your-competition rule he'd learned in journalism school. He found her intriguing. She treated every news story like she had a personal stake in it.

He pulled away from the crowd of police officers. The firemen had nearly gotten the blaze under control.

"Don't forget about hoops on Friday," one of the firemen shouted at his back.

"Yeah, sure." Who would have thought that playing basketball with the first responders would give him an in? They answered his phone calls and gave him inside info even when they were on the way to an emergency.

"See you then, Beck," said one of the other men.

He was still having trouble getting used to

responding to a last name that wasn't his. He didn't enjoy the deception, but it was the only way he could go back to living a normal life.

Over a year ago, he'd been reporting on the fighting in Syria when he was taken hostage by terrorists. Once he was released and back in the States, a lot of media attention had been directed his way. He wanted to cover the stories, not *be* the story. So he left Baltimore and came to Montana. Now he reported small-town news in a part of the world where it was easy enough to hide who he'd been. He didn't care where he lived as long as he could write and not have people asking him personal questions.

Zachery glanced back toward the crowd. His story was already wrapped up and posted by the time the other reporters were showing up. The only one who'd come close to being able to keep up with him was Elizabeth. Yet another thing he admired about her. But though he thought she was pretty and smart, he couldn't see their relationship getting beyond fun, professional competitiveness. Something about her demeanor suggested she was all about work. She had an aloofness to her he couldn't decipher.

What did it matter? After all the terror of his hostage experience, and then the ugly furor of the media frenzy, he needed time to put himself back together before he even thought of trying for some romance in his life.

He loved his job, and working to beat the pretty redhead to a story made him a better reporter. It was good for both of them, iron sharpening iron. Another news truck pulled into the lot, and Elizabeth's cameraman turned his attention to filming the police chief while he made his public statement.

Zach watched as a man in a hat disappeared around the corner of the building. A moment later, Elizabeth followed him.

A shiver, which had nothing to do with the night chill, ran over Zach's skin. Chalk it up to having spent so much time in war zones; his instincts for knowing when bad things were about to happen were finely honed. It wasn't a cognitive thing. His gut told him when danger was close. Right now, he didn't like the way his stomach clenched when Elizabeth disappeared around the corner of that building.

He shoved his phone in his pocket and dashed toward the shadowed darkness where Elizabeth had gone.

TWO

The illumination from the streetlights didn't reach to the back of the warehouse. Elizabeth's eyes probed the dark corners, trying to spot the man in the hat. Running wasn't always an indication of guilt, but her journalist curiosity wouldn't rest until she was sure the man was just an innocent bystander.

Her foot hit something hard and metal, sending a sharp pain up her leg. She stopped for a moment, pulled out her phone and switched on the flashlight at the end. The place looked like some sort of automobile graveyard. Piles of tires, bent metal and rusted-out cars populated the field.

She aimed the flashlight into the shadows. No sign or sound of the man anywhere. She would have seen him if he'd headed toward the well-lit street a hundred yards away, so he had to be here somewhere.

"Hey, I want to talk to you." The waver in

her voice gave away her fear. She stepped farther from the warehouse, shining the light all around. The sounds of the firefighters faded. Her pulse drummed in her ears.

What was she doing out here anyway? She couldn't waste any more time. She turned to head back to civilization when the creak of metal caught her attention. Her heart pounded against her rib cage.

"Hey," she said, edging toward where the noise had come from. "I just want to talk to you. Did you see something to do with the fire?"

Gravel crunched beneath her feet. Lifting her arm, she aimed the light at the shell of a car.

A hand went over her mouth. The smell of gasoline and dirt filled her nostrils.

Adrenaline shot through her body. She fought to twist free of her captor as memories of the assault she'd lived through in college bombarded her. She couldn't breathe. She couldn't see.

His arms were like iron around her waist as he pulled her through the field. She couldn't scream. She couldn't get away. She feared she might faint. How could this be happening again?

She dragged her feet.

"Stop it." His breath was like hot lava on her

skin. He pressed his mouth close to her ear. "I have a gun. Come with me or die."

Oh, please, dear God, no.

She took in a breath as she struggled to clear her head and get beyond the terror. Not only was her life in danger, her mind was drowning in the violent memories from ten years ago. But fighting back the fear was a familiar struggle—one she lived with almost every day. And this time, conquering her emotions might be the only way for her to stay alive.

"Stop resisting me."

The hard edge to her captor's words told her staying alive meant doing what he asked, for now. She stopped struggling. Her eyes scanned the dark landscape. There must be some way to save herself.

She trudged forward, turning to see the warehouse and the junk field in her peripheral vision. The lights looked a million miles away. Who was this man? Why was he doing this?

He poked the gun in her back. "Open the door."

A car materialized in front of her. They were on a dirt road behind the warehouse. Her hand reached out toward the handle.

She struggled to clear her mind of the horrifying images from ten years ago. Hands around her neck. Craig Miller grinning at her. She'd trusted him enough to go on a date with him.

Stay alive.

She fought to find her way back to this night and the new threat.

She knew from having covered abduction stories that once he had her in the car, her chances of getting away diminished.

He pressed close to her back, his clothes brushing against hers. She leaned forward as though to open the door but spun at the last moment, putting her head down and charging toward her abductor's chest.

The blow made him grunt, but he remained upright. He yanked her blazer collar. Cold metal pressed against her temple.

"I said get in." He pushed her hard against the car.

The impact knocked the wind out of her. She was shaking from the inside out as she reached for the car with a trembling hand and pulled open the door.

"Why are you doing this?"

"Wouldn't you like to know?" He jerked her hands behind her back and wrapped wire around her wrists before shoving her in the backseat and slamming the door shut behind her. Pain pulsed through her rib cage as she angled to sit up.

The driver's-side door opened. The man sat behind the wheel. The car roared to life. Nausea roiled through her stomach as black dots filled her vision. She struggled to remain coherent.

As the car sped through the darkness, she wondered if this time she would die.

Zachery's heart raced as he watched the dark figure push a woman into the car and speed off. That woman, who was probably Elizabeth, had clearly been abducted. He knew where that road led. He sprinted through the junkyard toward the side street where he'd parked his car, yanked open the door and jumped in. He thought to call the police but knew there wasn't time for them to get here and follow the car. He'd have to follow himself, and call it in once he found out where the man was going.

The engine revved to life, and he zigzagged down city streets to the edge of town, where pavement met gravel. Up ahead, he could see the red taillights of a car as it rolled over the hills out into the country. That had to be the guy. There were no other cars out this way.

Taillights winked out. The kidnapper knew he was being followed. Zach slowed his own car, trying to discern the shadows in front of him. Moonlight provided a hint of illumination as he came over the crest of a hill. He didn't see or hear any evidence of the car anywhere. His tires rolled silently over the dirt road.

After he drove for several minutes without seeing anything, he pulled over to the shoulder and got out. He saw no sign of a house or even a barn, no lights—no place where the man could have gone. Darkness consumed the road a couple of hundred yards ahead of him. To one side was a stretch of forest. Not even the mechanical clang of a distant car engine met his ears.

Time to call in one of his cop friends. He yanked on the car door.

Zach climbed back into his car, fumbling for his phone at the same time he turned the key in the ignition.

"Hey, Dan, it's Zach," he said as soon as the other man picked up. "I think I need your help. I'm out on Old Forsyth Road." He gave Dan the details of what he'd witnessed as he pulled out onto the road. He scanned three hundred and sixty degrees around him. He wasn't going to give up, and he wasn't going to wait for the police.

Whatever it took, he'd find the guy. There couldn't be that many roads out this way.

He turned onto a side road.

Backup would be nice when it arrived, but he couldn't wait around for it. A woman's life was at stake.

* * *

Hope rose up inside Elizabeth when her kidnapper switched off his lights. She turned her head and stared out the back window, seeing only shadows on the road. Someone must have seen the kidnapping and come after her. Why else would he turn off his lights?

As her body jostled on the seat from the car speeding down the road, Elizabeth wondered who had spotted them—maybe one of the police officers on the scene?

She lifted her head even as pain coiled around her rib cage and pulsated. "Why are you doing this?"

"You don't remember me, do you?"

A jolt of fear shot through her, and for a moment, she wondered if the man who had date raped her in college had come back to torment her. She shook off the rising terror. This man had a big build. Craig had been short and muscular. She'd remember her attacker's gravelly voice forever. She heard it in her dreams. This wasn't Craig Miller, the man who had nearly destroyed her, and the reason she had left a promising career in Seattle.

She struggled for breath as the memories flooded her mind.

Hold it together.

She stared at the back of his head. With

the baseball cap, she couldn't see his face or even what color his hair was. All she had to go on was that momentary connection she'd made when he'd been a face in the crowd. She couldn't even recall any of his features. "Where would I know you from?"

"Ha, nice try. The intrepid reporter always knows what questions to ask."

Even his voice wasn't distinctive. She twisted her hands, working the wires around her wrists loose.

Someone was looking for her. That gave her a fighting chance. All she had to do was stall for time. They drove for what felt like at least half an hour until he came to a stop. The back door cranked open, and he grabbed her arm just above the elbow. Squeezing hard, he yanked her out. She fell on the ground. Though the wire was now loose enough for her to slip free, she kept her hands behind her so her kidnapper wouldn't know.

"Before this night is over, you'll know who I am." His voice held menace that made her shiver.

She lifted her head, noticing the outline of a house. The broken window and dilapidated porch indicated it was abandoned.

"Get up." His words were filled with venom. She tried to push herself to her feet, but movement made her torso hurt. She must have broken or bruised a rib when he slammed her against the car. Each breath caused a stab of pain.

He grabbed her collar and pulled her to her feet, pressing his mouth close to her ear. "Don't even think of trying to escape." Violence undergirded each word.

Fear was like a thousand knives stabbing her vital organs. She couldn't get a deep breath. The same two words pounded over and over in her head.

Buy time. Buy time.

She could barely speak. "Please, I want to remember you. Have we met?"

He hesitated before pushing her. "Quit stalling."

His voice carried a nuance of emotion she hadn't heard before. She'd touched a nerve.

She purged her voice of the terror that gripped her. "Clearly, I was important to you. We have met." She managed a soft coyness in her tone.

"Stop. It." He spat the words out, but loosened his grip on her collar.

She detected weakness in his voice. She was getting to him.

She dared a look out on the dark horizon. Help should have arrived by now. Her stomach clenched. What if her kidnapper had only imagined he was being pursued? She hadn't seen any car lights.

Maybe it was up to her to escape on her own. She squeezed her eyes shut. *Think, Elizabeth. He's stronger than you, but he's not smarter.*

"It would be nice if we could talk. If you would just tell me why I matter to you." She chose her words carefully, struggling not to go into reporter mode. She wanted to know where this man knew her from, but the wrong sort of question might fuel his violence. Instead, she tried for an emotional connection to him.

His rough fingers rubbed against the vulnerable spot on her neck where he gripped her shirt collar.

His reaction was slow in coming as though he were processing what she had said. Did he realize she was manipulating him?

"Elizabeth Kramer, big-time reporter." He expelled the words in a single breath as though he'd been punched in the stomach. "You're just so smart, aren't you?"

She kept her voice to a soft whisper, hoping that would persuade him. "Why can't we talk? Can you tell me your first name?"

He tightened his grip on her neck. Panic shot through her like a bullet. She'd overplayed her hand.

"You should know who I am." His words dripped with indignation.

"Really, why?" Talking to him didn't seem to be helping, but she refused to let the fear win. She would get away no matter what it took. Her father had taught her how to defend herself.

While he was distracted by her question, she leaned against him and rammed her elbow into his stomach. He grunted. The grip on her neck loosened. She burst forward and angled to the side, wriggling her hands free from the wire. In the darkness, she could feel his hands on her, grasping, trying to get a hold.

Keep fighting.

She stumbled forward into the dark forest. He grabbed her shirt at the hem, yanked her back. She turned and smashed her flat palm against where she thought his face was. Skin smacked against skin.

She ran again, his footsteps at her heels. She could make out very little in the darkness. The roughness of the terrain told her she wasn't on a road or trail. If she could get back to the car, maybe he'd left the keys in the ignition.

Her heart raged in her chest as she zigzagged, turning in a wide circle back to where they'd been. The sound of his footsteps dimmed. She ran faster.

The abandoned house came into view. She

slowed her pace. No human noise reached her ears. The trees thinned, becoming more like bushes. She crouched lower.

She slipped out from behind a bush. Still bent over, she started toward where she remembered the car being. The landscape was nothing more than shadows.

She peered through the darkness, trying to discern objects. No car. She must have come around to the back of the house. A branch broke off to the side of her. Desperate to hide, she scrambled toward the house, slipped inside and pressed against a rough wooden wall. The drumming of her heart in her ear threatened to drown out all other sound.

She still couldn't see the car through the window. It must be on the other side of the trees.

She crouched on the floor, working her way toward the door. Her eyes adjusted enough so she could make out the outline of an object on the floor. She crawled toward it, careful not to make the floorboards creak.

Her hand reached out, touching the cold metal of a chain. The air left her lungs with a whoosh as a chill struck the marrow of her bones. Groping in the dark, she followed the chain to a set of manacles at the end. Her lungs compressed. The abduction had been planned. He was going to keep her as a prisoner here.

A foot padded on wood. She whirled around to see a hulking figure in the doorway.

She opened her mouth to speak, but no words came out. Terror embedded deep into her muscles. She couldn't move.

He pounded across the floor, grabbed her by the elbows and lifted her up.

"Don't you dare try to get away from me." Rage colored every word.

Spit hit her face. His anger gave her the will to fight. Even though her ribs hurt, she kicked and twisted her body. But it was no use. His arm didn't budge from around her waist. A claw-like hand grabbed her hair, rendering her immobile.

Below her, the chain glistened in the moonlight.

"I want to know...what I did to you. I want to make it right."

"Liar." He tossed her to floor, the impact sending reverberations up her knees and agony through her ribs. He reached for the chain. She crawled on all fours to get away, but he grabbed for her. His grip on her ankle was like iron.

She could feel herself shutting down and the world going black as ten-year-old memories crashed in from all sides.

Oh, God, help me.

Adrenaline coursed through her like a raging river of fire. She was not going to be his prisoner. And she was not going to die out here. She clenched her teeth, flipped over and kicked with her free leg.

Bright lights shone suddenly through the broken glass of the window. A car was coming down the hill toward the house.

He let go of her ankle, grabbed her at the shoulders and pulled her close.

"Looks like the cavalry is here. But that doesn't mean you're safe. Just remember, the next time you go to a story, it might be me who created it to lure you there. You will never feel safe again."

His words seemed to linger in the air even as his footsteps pounded across the floor. She sat stunned. A car engine started up outside.

Footsteps pounded toward her. Arms surrounded her and lifted her from the floor.

"It's going to be all right, Elizabeth. I'm here. The police are on their way." Zach's voice reverberated softly in her ear.

She pressed close to his chest and thanked God Zach had found her.

THREE

Zachery placed the steaming cup of coffee in Elizabeth's hand while the activity of the police station buzzed around them.

He pressed his hand against hers, making sure she had a grip on the cup. "Probably not the tastiest, but it will warm you up."

Elizabeth stared straight ahead, not focusing on anything. His heart squeezed tight with empathy. This was not the same confident woman he enjoyed bantering with. He'd seen the same effect on soldiers. The violence she'd witnessed must have stripped her bare, left every emotion raw and exposed and turned her brain into shredded mush.

"Go ahead, have a sip. I put three sugars in it." His hand still covered hers. He feared she would drop the coffee if he pulled away.

She drew the cup to her lips. He sat in the hard plastic chair beside her. He couldn't leave her, not in the state she was in.

"It's not too bad." She stared down into the steaming liquid. "Thank you." She spoke in a monotone.

He knew the thank-you was for more than the bad coffee. "My pleasure." He glanced around at the officer assigned to her case, who typed away on his keyboard. "Busy night. I'm sure he'll be able to take your statement soon." When the cop glanced up from his keyboard, Zach offered him a raised eyebrow as if to say *hurry up*.

The night had been long enough already. Elizabeth had gone through a medical exam that revealed she had bruised ribs.

Another policeman walked by them, punching Zach in the shoulder as he passed.

She lifted her chin. "Do you know everyone in this town, Beck? You haven't lived here that long."

Her voice still lacked the old fight he'd gotten used to, but at least she was feeling well enough to take a shot at him.

"What can I say, people just gravitate toward this handsome mug of mine." He rubbed his chin.

She shook her head. "Yeah, right, that must be it." Her smile faded and she gazed back into her coffee cup.

The brief moment of humor passed, and a

taut silence coiled around them. What had happened to her out there in that house? He knew more than he wanted to about the terror connected with being abducted.

Experience on a very personal level told him what she needed. "I'll stay," he said.

"What?"

"I'll stay while you give your statement…if you want me to." He didn't want to seem forward. "Or I can call someone."

"There's no one to call. I have friends but… my father is really the only one I would want here. He died a few years ago," she said. "I moved back here from Seattle, then he got sick and I took care of him at the end."

"Sorry about your dad." He was surprised to hear there was no one else important in her life, though. A beautiful, smart woman and no boyfriend to call? He mentally kicked himself. Why was he even entertaining that thought? The last thing on his radar was a girlfriend. "It's settled, then. You're stuck with me, Betsy."

"Is that right?" She picked a piece of invisible lint off her jacket. "I guess this means I owe you."

"You don't owe me anything," he said. And he meant that.

"That's not the way I see it. I'll find a way to

repay you. I can't give you some sort of scoop on a story because you always beat me to them already. But I'll think of something."

The police officer rose to his feet. "Miss Kramer. Sorry for the delay. I'm ready to take your statement now."

She took in a sharp breath, and her back stiffened. It was clear she dreaded having to relive everything she'd just been through.

He wanted to wrap an arm around her, to calm her, but instead he pressed his shoulder against hers. "It's going to be okay."

The look she gave him was one of utter confusion, like she couldn't process what he'd just said.

She rose from her chair and walked toward the officer's desk. Zach stood behind her.

"Have they been able to find the man?" Her hand curled into a fist and her voice faltered.

"We've got units patrolling the woods. We're dusting that house for prints along with the..." the officer cleared his throat "...the items that we found inside."

Zach had seen the manacles and chains on the floor. At least he'd been able to keep her from being held prisoner.

Images of his own captivity infected his thoughts. After a brutal beating, he was thrown in a small room that smelled like urine. The room had no windows. Though he lived in constant fear, it was only after he was free that he learned the terrorist group had filmed the beheading of two other reporters and that he had been next in line to die.

If it hadn't been for the dauntless work of his sister, his life could have ended, as well. The reality of how close he'd been to death brought him back to the God he'd loved as a teenager.

The officer looked up at Elizabeth. "Miss Kramer, are you ready to answer the questions?"

Zach watched as Elizabeth swayed backward. Fearing she might faint, he held out his hand to catch her. She righted herself and squared her shoulders.

She touched her fingers to her lips. When she spoke, it was in her reporter's voice. "Clearly, it was premeditated and personal. The guy acted like I should know who he was."

She needed to distance herself from the terror of the attack. He understood the coping mechanism.

"Let's get started with the interview so we can catch this guy." The officer stared at Zach.

"He has my permission to stay," said Elizabeth. Warmth filled her eyes when she looked over at him.

Maintaining her reporter persona, she answered the officer's questions. Zach watched her, her gaze never wavering, her voice like sharpened steel. He didn't know her whole life's story, but he admired her inner strength. She wasn't allowing herself to falter, even if it meant pretending the abduction had happened to someone else.

When the interview was over, Zach turned to her. "I can take you home."

"Thanks," she said. "I'd appreciate it. I'm sure Dale took the van back to the news station. I'll call him and let him know I'm okay when I get home."

They walked down the long hallway that led to the outside, their shoes tapping on the concrete floor. He held the door open for her.

A male news reporter scurried over to them.

"Oh, great. Neil Thompson, my prime competition," Elizabeth said under her breath.

Neil shoved the microphone toward Elizabeth. "So, Miss Kramer, you had quite an ordeal tonight."

"Please, I don't want to talk…" She looked like she would crumple to the pavement.

Neil persisted. "Have they caught the man who abducted you?"

His ire rising, Zach wrapped an arm around Elizabeth's shoulders and guided her toward the parking lot.

Neil's words pelted their backs. "How does it feel to be the story instead of covering it, Elizabeth?"

Zach felt an echo of his own life in the question. Maybe he could help Elizabeth get through this. "Don't give him anything to feed off of. The story will die down in a couple of days if you don't give them anything."

She pressed close to him, seeking his protection. Neil traipsed after them with his cameraman in tow.

"I know the public has a short attention span. It's just going to be a long couple of days." Frustration colored her words.

Zach turned to face Neil, holding his palm toward the other reporter. "She really doesn't want to talk right now." Zach kept his voice level.

They were within a few feet of his car. He reached over to the passenger side door. Elizabeth slipped into the seat.

He was about to close the door when Neil bent down and leaned close to Elizabeth. "Did the events of tonight bring back what happened to you in college?"

Elizabeth's face went completely white. "How…did you…find out about that?" Not giving him a chance to answer, she grabbed the door and slammed it.

Zach resisted the urge to push Neil. His hands curled into fists. "You need to leave right now." He had no idea what events Neil was referencing, but the comment clearly had upset Elizabeth.

Neil put up his hand in a surrender gesture. "A story is a story."

Despite his warm onscreen persona, Neil Thompson always struck Zach as being a little slimy. Now he seemed downright repellent. "Is that what it's really about or are you just trying to humiliate your competition?"

Neil shook his head. "Just trying to do my job."

"I doubt that." He brushed past Neil, close enough that Neil had to take a step back. "Get out of my way and stay out of hers."

Zach yanked open the driver's-side door and got behind the wheel. Elizabeth still looked pale, and her mouth was drawn into a hard, flat line. She turned her face toward the window when he glanced over at her.

As he pulled out of the parking lot, he got a view of Neil and his cameraman, both with angry expressions. He was glad to see them growing smaller and farther away in the rearview mirror.

Elizabeth continued to stare out the window. Whatever Neil had made a reference to, it had cut Elizabeth to the core. His heart ached for her. He liked Neil Thompson even less. Getting the story was one thing. Deliberately hurting someone was another thing entirely. "You don't have to tell me what he was talking about. Let's just get you home."

Still burning from what Neil Thompson had brought up, Elizabeth's hand trembled when she flipped through her keys to find the one for her house. As they pulled up to the curb, her home was a welcome sight. They got out of the car and made their way up the walk.

A familiar looking woman parked at the curb exited her car and bustled toward Elizabeth— Gwen Monroe from the *Badger Chronicle*. Elizabeth's knees felt weak. The bombardment just kept coming. She really didn't want to deal with this right now or at any time. She liked being the one doing the interview.

Zachery stepped between Elizabeth and the woman. "Gwen, she doesn't want to talk to anyone."

Gwen lifted her chin. "A well-known reporter gets kidnapped. That's a story, Zach."

After shoving the key in the lock, Elizabeth breathed a prayer of thanks for Zach. The man was her nemesis in so many ways. But he'd come through for her when she needed him most. In the days to come, she knew she would need all the friends she could get, especially if other reporters kept circling around.

She was still bothered that Neil Thompson had found out about her date rape. The case had never made it to trial, but the allegations had been covered by the college newspaper and her name had been leaked. Still, it wasn't like it had been front page news. Neil didn't strike her as the investigative reporter type either.

Zach's voice held authority as he faced Gwen. "Find a different story. She's not ready to make any kind of a statement."

Gwen took several steps back.

Elizabeth pushed open the door and closed her eyes. "Stay," she said to Zach. Her words held a desperation she hadn't expected.

"What?"

"Stay until we're sure there are no more reporters going to bother me." Normally, she wouldn't even be comfortable asking a man into her house. But Zach seemed...safe.

He met her gaze, and for the first time, she noticed that his eyes were more gray than blue.

"I can do that." He nodded before glancing over his shoulder. "Gwen doesn't give up easily."

Elizabeth slipped inside her house, and he followed. She hit the light switch by the door.

Nothing had changed in her living room, though it felt like an entirely different place. She was not the same person who had left here to cover the warehouse fire.

The warm tones of the living room that normally looked so cozy only made her feel more alone.

"How about I make you some tea?" Zach offered.

"Let me. It's my kitchen." She moved toward the counter.

He touched her arm just above the elbow. "No, you need to sit down. I'll figure out where things are in the kitchen."

Though his touch was gentle, his words held force. She didn't have the energy to argue with him.

"Thanks for everything. Now I double owe you," she said.

"It's all part of my evil plan. Soon you will owe me the world." He rubbed his hands together theatrically and laughed like a villain in a cartoon.

In spite of everything, he made her shake her head and smile. When she laughed, her ribs hurt, just a reminder that the bruising would take weeks to heal.

"There's that beauty queen toothy grin we all adore, Betsy," he teased.

She rolled her eyes, amazed at how easily he could pull her from a dark place with his humor. "Stop—it was one pageant and winning paid for journalism school." She'd been only eighteen then. Small town girl headed to the big city, so full of hope. She slumped down on the couch and watched as he put a teakettle on and opened cupboards to find cups and tea.

She was grateful he hadn't pressed for details about what happened in college. Craig Miller had never gone to jail. Her lawyer had believed her, but there hadn't been enough evidence. The trauma of the attack had caused her to fall apart emotionally, which would have made her a bad witness. She understood why the case hadn't gone to trial, but the fact that she'd never gotten closure made it hard to move on emotionally. Her trust toward men had been completely broken. She had decided not to date and put her energy into her work. "I do want to pay you back some way."

"Don't worry about it," he said.

"You seem to be old hat at fending off the press. Like you've been through it before."

He opened a tea bag and placed it in a cup. "Do I?"

She caught the hitch in his voice, the way he froze for a nanosecond before opening the tea bag. He wasn't telling her the whole story.

She'd done enough interviews to pick up on the subtle clues and body language that he was hiding something. Fear skittered across her nerves. Her back stiffened. She hoped she hadn't been foolish to let him in.

The kettle whistled, and he turned his back to her before she could read his expression. When he swung around again, it was as if he was wearing a mask. He poured the tea and brought the cup over to her, taking a seat in the chair across from her.

So they both had secrets. She took the steaming mug and raised it. "To the giver of hot beverages."

She studied him over the top of her mug. She had a feeling that even if she probed a little more, Zach would not be forthcoming. His keen reporter instincts would clue him in that she was turning him into an interview subject. A Google search would probably be more productive.

"You're not going to have any tea?"

"I'm the giver of hot beverages, not the drinker," he said.

She took a sip, allowing the warm liquid to flow down her throat while the minty flavor lingered on her tongue. "Nothing like tea to soothe the rankled soul."

He nodded. "I suppose."

The reporter in her really wanted to know what he was hiding. She studied him long enough that he started to fidget. He burst up from his seat opposite her, turning his back to her and shoving his hands in his pockets.

"So have you ever had to fend off the press?" she finally asked.

He offered her a nervous smile. "Don't go all journalist on me, Betsy. I thought we had a pretty good start on being friends."

Friends? She hadn't thought about that possibility.

He stared out the window. "Looks like Gwen is gone."

His changing the subject told her she'd pushed a little too far. "I should be okay here alone." The idea caused a new wave of fear to crash over her.

"You'll be safe from the reporters, but…"

He seemed to understand her trauma in a way that others would not have been so sensitive to.

"Tell you what, why don't you try to sleep," he offered. "I'll grab my laptop and get some work done."

Zach seemed completely trustworthy, but trusting too easily was what had gotten her in trouble in college. "Really, you've done so much already."

"It's not that big a deal. I was only going to go home and sit with my laptop there."

She did want him to stay. She wasn't ready to face being in the house alone. "I don't know if I could sleep, but maybe both of us could get some work done."

"All right, then." He moved toward the door but stopped when something on the entryway table caught his eye. "You're going to the Waltz by the River Ball?"

She rose to her feet. "Yes, part of being a good reporter these days is keeping in touch with the movers and shakers." Badger was a community of fifty thousand, so there weren't that many muckety-mucks, as her father used to call them, to rub elbows with.

"If you could swing me an invitation, I'd consider us even. Since you're so convinced you owe me," he said.

"Sure. Actually, I need a date." It was hardly a fair trade, considering he'd saved her life. "Why do you want to go?"

"You get better stories when people recognize your face," he said. "Since I'm new in town, I've got to start making connections with those people."

So he had an in with the first responders, but not the power brokers like she did. She chided herself for thinking in terms of them competing, though it came so naturally. She walked across the floor and placed her teacup on the counter. "You do realize this is a formal party."

"I can rent a tux." He stroked his five-o'clock shadow and yanked open the door.

"You'll have to locate a razor, too."

"Yeah, yeah." He stepped outside after offering her a playful backward glare.

Shaking her head, she watched him stride toward his car. He came back a moment later holding his laptop. They sat on opposite sides of the living room, the tapping of the keys the only sound in the house. Though they were working on separate projects, the sense of companionship was kind of nice. After about twenty minutes, her eyelids felt heavy. She placed the laptop on the side table. "Maybe I'll just rest my eyes."

"Sleep is the best thing for you now." His voice was soft and far away.

She heard him get up, and a moment later, the creamy softness of the couch throw enveloped her.

As she drifted off, she wondered why a man who seemed so forthright like Zachery would have something to hide.

She felt herself falling into a deeper sleep. Images of the abduction blasted through her dreams. She awoke with a start, jerking into a sitting position.

Zach seemed alarmed. "Everything all right?" His voice filled with sympathy.

She rose to her feet and turned away. "I'm fine." What a lie. Her abductor's threat to lure her to another news story so he could take her again made her throat go tight and her heart race. She wouldn't be safe until he was caught.

FOUR

Despite the warm summer air, a chill crawled over Elizabeth's skin as she got out of Zach's car. Seeing the crowd moving through the parking lot toward the country club where Waltz by the River was being held only made her more anxious. This was the first public event she'd been to since her abduction. Her stomach knotted. All these people. Any one of them could be the man who'd kidnapped her.

Zach came up beside her, pressing his shoulder against hers. "Lots of hoity-toity people."

The warmth of his voice calmed her. "Yes, I'm amazed they let the likes of us in." She glanced over at him, clean-shaven and wearing a tux. Though his blond hair still looked a little out of control, he did clean up nicely.

His hand lightly touched the middle of her back. "Let's go mingle, shall we?"

His touch made her afraid and excited at the same time. She'd given up on dating after what happened her senior year of college. But she found herself relaxing around Zach. "I'll introduce you to the mayor." She lifted the skirt of her gown as they both ascended the wide staircase.

Music spilled from the open doors of the country club, which looked out on a river on one side and was surrounded by a golf course on the other three.

Tension twisted around her chest as the noise of people in party mode grew louder. She studied each face. What was she looking for anyway? Some sign of guilt? Maybe there was nothing to find. The man might have already left town. Yet, his threat to lure her to a story to get another shot at her fed her paranoia.

She wasn't here to cover a story. Her boss at the station had given her a week off to recover from the trauma. Other than to get groceries, she hadn't left the house at all. Her heart raced as a man she knew loomed toward her.

Richard Drake, owner of several businesses, held out his hand. "Elizabeth, so good to see you."

An uncomfortable silence filled the air between them. She saw in his eyes that he knew what had happened to her. Even though she'd followed Zach's advice and not done interviews, her story had been in print and on the local news. Only Zach had chosen not to write about it.

Elizabeth took Richard's hand. "So good to see you here." She turned toward Zach. "This is Zachery Beck. I'm sure you have heard about his news blog."

Richard's eyes brightened. "Ah yes, who would have thought one man could steal so much readership from the *Badger Chronicle*." His voice held a note of animosity.

"Richard is part owner in the *Chronicle*," she explained to Zach.

Richard shook Zach's hand a moment too long. "You and I should talk about a partnership."

"I like my independence," said Zach.

Richard raised an eyebrow. "I'm sure you do." Offense colored his words. He turned away and headed toward a huddle of men.

She spoke under her breath and elbowed him. "I thought you wanted to network, Zach, not make enemies."

"I've never been very good at that," he said. "And I have no interest in being bought out or controlled by some corporate entity."

"You should at least try not to burn bridges before they're even built," she said. "Both of you are in the same business. It wouldn't kill you to be cordial."

He let out a breath. "Sorry, I'm not the king of diplomacy. That seems to be your gift. Maybe you can help me with that."

The music swelled, and they turned toward the dance floor as it filled with couples. He grabbed her hand before she had time to protest and whirled her out there.

Trepidation crept in. Dancing meant touching in a sustained way, which always made her nervous. "I'm not much of a dancer," she said.

He offered her a disarming smile. "It beats networking." He took her hand.

His touch was disarming.

As the waltz played, his hand warmed the middle of her back. She cupped his shoulder. For the first time in ten years, she was allowing a man other than her father to touch her for any length of time. Dancing was safe. At least that's what she told herself, but butterflies in her stomach relayed another story.

He circled her around the dance floor with ease. As the song played, she found herself relaxing just a little. He was such a good dancer, she didn't even have to think about the steps.

She whirled around and then looked at him. His blue, almost gray eyes blazed through her, and she thought she saw just a hint of affection there. The idea made her heart flutter, but she pulled away as the song ended as fear invaded her awareness.

He seemed to instinctually know that he shouldn't touch her. Instead, he stood close to her. "Sorry, networking made me nervous. I needed to escape."

She walked toward the food table, grabbing a glass and filling it with punch. "Where did you learn how to dance like that?" Her heart was still racing as she handed him the drink.

"Believe it or not, knowing how to waltz got me a contact I needed for a story years ago." He took a sip of his drink.

"Oh, really, where was that?"

"Baltimore." His jawline went taut. Clearly, he didn't like it when she probed about his past. Her journalist mind just couldn't let go of the idea that he was hiding something.

She poured herself a drink and then tilted her glass toward a corner of the room. "The mayor is over there. Would you like to take a shot at diplomacy again?"

His back stiffened. "Maybe later. Can you excuse me for just a moment? Point me in the direction of the restroom."

Elizabeth shook her head as she watched him cross the room. After saying hello to several people, her nerves were on edge. Being in public was harder than she'd been prepared for.

She found herself wishing for Zach's return. Nobody mentioned the abduction directly, but the body language of the people she spoke to suggested a certain level of discomfort.

Neil Thompson's laughter rose above the murmur as he slapped the back of one of the men he was with. He started to turn in her direction. She panicked. The last person she wanted to talk to was Neil.

She hurried over to an out-of-the-way table by the kitchen and sat down. Her view of the room was slightly obscured, and noise from the kitchen overpowered the party chatter. She took in a deep breath, hoping to stop her racing heart. She really wasn't ready yet to be out in public. Only Zach's presence had made it bearable, and without him by her side, she felt overwhelmed.

"Excuse me, miss." A waiter stood beside her table. "A man asked me to give you this." He placed a folded piece of paper on the table and walked away.

She picked it up and unfolded it. In bold type the note said *I am watching you.*

Her breath caught. She jerked to her feet and glanced around at the crowd of people. No one looked in her direction. By the time she stepped outside to catch a breath of fresh air and get away from the crowd, anxiety raged through her.

She crossed her arms over her body. She needed to go home now. Or maybe she needed to talk to the police chief. He was here tonight. In her haste to leave the ballroom, she'd dropped the note. She gazed out on the dark river, allowing the rushing water to calm her. Her phone buzzed, indicating she had a text. The noise startled her.

Her fingers trembled as she unclipped the fastener on her clutch and pulled out her phone. Was the stalker texting her now? She pressed the button that opened up her texts. Zach. She let out the breath she'd been holding and read.

Where R U?

She saw him through the glass wall that separated the balcony from the ballroom. He looked up from his phone, his expression changing. He must have seen something on her face even at this distance.

He stepped outside and moved toward her. "Elizabeth, what is it?"

She could barely get the words out. "He's… here."

Zach stepped closer to her. "Who? You mean the man who… How do you know?"

"A waiter brought me a note that said…" She swallowed. "He was watching me."

"Where is the note?"

She looked at her empty hands. "I must have dropped it." She'd been so upset, she wasn't thinking straight.

"Do you remember what the waiter looked like?"

She stared through the glass wall. All the waiters were dressed the same in white shirts and black pants. "I think if I saw him I might."

He cupped her elbow. "Let's go back in there."

She took in a ragged breath. *He's in there watching me.*

Zach's soft tone indicated that he'd picked up on her fear. "I'll stay with you the whole time. You want this guy put away, don't you?"

She nodded, took in a breath and steeled herself against the fear.

"We'll just walk around the room."

He stepped inside with her. She studied not only the waiters but the other guests, looking for any sign of menace as she skirted the edges the ballroom and then threaded between the tables. She had a vague memory of the waiter's short dark hair…and glasses. He had glasses. "That's him." She pointed to a waiter headed through the swinging doors that led to the kitchen.

Zach grabbed her hand, and they hurried across the floor. A cacophony of noise assaulted them as they entered the humid kitchen. Cooks shouting at each other cooks, waiters shouting at cooks, pans banging, food sizzling and water running.

Zach caught the waiter as he picked up a plate. "Did you give this woman a note earlier?"

The waiter studied Elizabeth for a moment and then nodded. "The news lady. I didn't realize it was you."

Elizabeth stepped toward him. She purged her voice of any fear and switched on to reporter mode. "Can you describe the man who gave you the note?"

The waiter shrugged. "I look at a thousand faces in a night, taking orders from all of them." He shook his head.

"Can't you remember anything?"

"Sorry, I can't help you." He made his way toward the swinging door.

Disappointment saturated Zach's voice. "Come on, I'll take you home."

"Let's go back to the table. Maybe the note is still there." There might be fingerprints on it or something that would help the police track her tormentor.

A quick search revealed that the note was not to be found. She was mad at herself for having dropped it. She didn't like being rattled like that. Usually, she was pretty levelheaded.

"Let's blow this popsicle stand." Zach led her toward the door.

She scanned the sea of faces one more time before leaving the ballroom. Neil Thompson locked her in his gaze and stalked toward her.

She walked faster. "Let's get out of here before he has a chance to dive-bomb me."

As they hurried outside, the sharp heaviness of terror sunk through her skin and permeated to the bone. It was a fear she knew would be her strange companion until the man who had abducted her was behind bars.

Zach glanced over his shoulder. Just as their feet hit the bottom stair, Neil Thompson came outside. "That guy just never gives up."

Elizabeth wrapped her arm through Zach's. "The last thing I want to do is answer his questions."

She stood close enough for him to catch a hint of her citrus perfume.

He stared out at the sea of cars, trying to remember where he'd parked. There had been fewer cars out here when they'd pulled up. He headed in the general direction he thought his might be.

She followed him. "Don't tell me. You don't remember where you parked."

"Sorry," he said.

"I do it all the time," she said.

Even though she was being very forgiving, he picked up on the nervous tremble in her voice. The note had clearly shaken her. He flirted with the idea that the note was not connected to the abduction, just some sick person having fun with a local celebrity. It was possible...but not very likely.

Elizabeth walked beside him through the dark parking lot, lifting her skirt so it didn't drag on the concrete. "Weren't we more toward the seventh hole?" She indicated a section of the golf course that bordered the parking lot.

Dark shadows covered her the farther away they got from the warm glow of the country club. She'd looked so beautiful on the dance floor, the flush of color in her cheeks, eyes sparkling with life. Red-blond hair swept up into a bun. It was the first time he'd seen her happy since all of this had happened. That happy smile was gone now, replaced with a tense, worried frown.

They made their way through the dark lot. "I wonder if I'm ever going to be able to go out in public."

His heart went out to her. He remembered feeling like a prisoner in his sister's home because of the press hounding him. If he could catch the guy, he'd throttle him with his bare hands for doing this to her. What was his game anyway? "We've got a good police force. They will catch him."

"I don't see your car anywhere. Do you have a panic button on your key fob?"

"No, my car is old," he said.

"It's so dark out here. How about I do that row, and you walk that way? Shout when you find it," she said over her shoulder as she trotted away.

She walked in one direction and he in the other. He could kick himself for not paying closer attention to where he'd parked. The truth was he'd been focused on how beautiful Elizabeth had looked and trying not to sound like an idiot when he talked to her. Nothing could come of it. Theirs had been a date of convenience. He reminded himself of his vow to pull himself together before he even considered a relationship. Besides, as soon as she went back to work, they'd be back to knocking each other down to get to a news story again.

Finally, his nondescript, forgettable car came into view. One row over. He lifted his head and turned a half circle. "I found it." He didn't see Elizabeth anywhere. Almost no artificial light made it to this part of the parking lot. "Elizabeth?"

His chest squeezed tight as though it were in a vise. He jogged past the cars in the direction she'd been walking. His jog turned into an all out sprint.

Then he heard it, faint and far away, a scream from the golf course green. He took off running as he recognized Elizabeth's voice.

FIVE

Elizabeth saw only flashes of light and color as the man dragged her across the green. Her pumps had fallen off in the struggle, and her feet brushed over the wet grass. He had her in a neck lock with one arm while the other was wrapped around her waist, pulling her sideways.

She could barely breathe or move. He'd waited until she was close to the edge of the parking lot and then grabbed her. One thought crashed over another. How was she going to get away? If she could scream again, Zach might hear it.

She lifted her hands and scratched at his forearm. The action only made him tighten his grip around her neck. In the night sky, clouds and stars pulsated above her as she tried to twist free of his hold on her.

Her kidnapper descended a small hill and the country club faded from view. His grip loosened, shifted as he hefted her fully into his arms...and then threw her. She sailed through the air and landed in a shallow pool. Water surged around her. He lunged toward her. She angled to get away, but the weight of her wet dress made it hard to move.

He clamped onto her shoulders and pushed her under. She clawed at his hands as she took in water. He jerked her up. She gasped for air.

Though she could not make out any features in the dark, his face was very close to hers. "Are you scared yet?" His words cut her to the core.

Still gripping her at the shoulder, he cranked his head sideways and cursed. Something had alarmed him.

He dumped her in the pond. "I'm not done with you yet. Remember that." He took off running; his footsteps barely registered on the soft grass.

"Elizabeth!" Zach's voice sounded so far away.

Air filled her lungs and she tried to pull herself out of the water. "Here, I'm here." Her words came out as barely a whisper.

He called for her again.

She summoned strength somewhere deep inside and managed to shout. "Zach, I'm over here."

He was beside her within a few seconds,

pulling her to her feet. She fell against him, holding on tight and shaking. No words came. She wrapped her arms around his neck grateful for his strength and silence. He held her close. Her whole body was shaking.

After a long moment, she said, "He got away."

"I've called into the police station. They'll do a search. And since I didn't dial 911, we might be able to avoid other reporters picking it up on their police scanners. I'm sure you don't want to be a news item again."

"Thank you." Her cheek rested against his chest as gratitude flowed through her. She touched his sleeve. "I'm sorry, I got you all wet."

He waved his hand in the air to indicate it didn't matter. "Let's go down to the police station and file a report."

Anxiety surged up her throat. "Please, I can't. I just want to go home, where it's safe."

"Okay, maybe later," he said. "They can contact you after they've finished their search."

There was a part of her that didn't believe the police would do anything helpful. Past experience told her that you didn't always get justice where the law was concerned. She took a wobbly step out of the water, weighted down by her soaked dress. He wrapped an arm around her waist.

When they got back to the parking lot, a few more people were already leaving. She pressed in close to him, not wanting to be seen or have to explain what had happened. She rested her head against his neck so no one would recognize her.

He seemed to instinctually know what she needed.

She could feel the weight of a few stares as Zach opened the passenger side door for her.

Zach got in and pulled out of the lot and was on the country road back into town in a few short minutes. As fields and fences clipped by, she wondered who her attacker was. His question lingered in her mind.

Are you scared yet?

Very different from the first attack when he insisted that she should know who he was.

He had had opportunity to drown her and instead had dragged the torture out. Who was he? What did he want from her?

Only his tight grip on the steering wheel gave away how angry Zach was. He was angry at himself for letting his guard down. He never should have let Elizabeth wander the parking lot alone. And he was enraged at the attacker. If he could get his hands on that guy...

Zach took in a breath. Violence never solved anything, and the last thing Elizabeth needed was to see his rage. Though it wasn't directed at her, she had witnessed enough for one night.

They passed several police cars headed toward the country club on their way back into town. He'd asked the officers to keep it low-key for Elizabeth's sake.

What he needed to do was direct his angry energy at finding this stalker. "Any idea who this guy might be? Why he's after you?"

She took a moment to answer and then spoke slowly as though she were processing all that had happened. "Last time, he was angry at me for not knowing who he is and this time, he said he wants me to be scared." Her voice wavered a little, probably from having to revisit what she'd just been through. "He's inconsistent."

She was holding it together pretty well, but he knew he had to be careful with his questions. Everyone had a breaking point, and he didn't want to find hers. "So maybe it's connected to a news story you did or a crazed fan," he said.

She let out a little laugh. "I'm a reporter on a regional station. How many fans do you think I have?"

"To some people, anybody who is on television is famous. You must get fan mail."

"Nothing scary or obsessive. Not even back when I worked for the larger station in Seattle," she said.

When he'd researched her, he remembered thinking it was strange to give up a big-city job to come here. "Badger is a step down from Seattle."

She laced her hands together. "I came back here to take care of my father." He detected just a hint of defensiveness in her response.

Her father had died only few years ago. Clearly, she wasn't telling the whole story. He let it go. She'd talk about it when she wanted to…or never. It was her choice. He certainly was in no position to judge when it came to keeping secrets.

She turned slightly in her seat to face him. "I don't want to talk about Seattle. We both have to quit acting like reporters if we're going to work on being friends."

The lights of Badger came into view as he rolled down the two-lane. It was a fragile friendship. They were both a little too good at reading other people, and they both had a hard time shutting off the journalist instincts. Still, he warmed to the idea. Friends he could handle. "Agreed. I'll try my best."

He did like the idea of being her friend instead of her competition.

She nodded. "Okay, so let's problem solve here."

"Maybe this stalker is connected to a news story you covered," he said.

She stared through the windshield as though a video were playing before her eyes. "There was one guy about five years ago. Randy Smith. He went to jail for robbery. He threatened everyone who had anything to do with his trial." She touched the skirt of her ruined ball gown. "I remember, he pointed directly at me in the courtroom. I was only doing my job and reporting the facts."

"That has to have been scary," Zach said.

"It was, but I helped see that justice was the outcome and that made me feel good," she said.

He slowed down when they entered the Badger city limits. So she desired justice over her own safety. He realized then he was sitting beside a very brave woman. "So would he be out by now?"

"I think so. And if I'm remembering right, he had a similar build to the guy who attacked me." She cleared her throat and then rubbed her forehead. Her shoulders slumped. "I know this is important, and I want to get to bottom of it, but I really don't want to think about this right now."

He nodded. He wanted to nab this guy—Elizabeth wouldn't be safe until they did—but it was clear the trauma was catching up to her. He slowed as he drew close to her neighborhood. He pulled up to the curb and pushed open his door. He ran around to her side of the car and held out a hand for her.

Even if she looked composed on the outside, he was pretty sure she was in a wrestling match with deep fear on the inside. Her fingers were cool to the touch as she gave him only a passing glance.

At the door, she fumbled through her clutch for the keys. She unlocked the door and pushed it open. She turned to face him.

"Thank you, Zach." She reached up and touched his face. The brush of her hand on his cheek was so fleeting he thought he might have imagined it. The sudden heat on his face and the tight throat told him he hadn't.

"No problem, Betsy." The remark was intended to put distance between them. Her touch and his response to it caught him off-guard. They were still working on becoming friends, right? Nothing more. "I'll let you know what the cops find out." He'd do anything to pull her from the pit of angst she must be in. "You going to be all right?"

"I really just want to go into my house, lock the doors and not think about this right now."

He understood all too well needing to block out everything.

She stepped inside and shut the door. He hurried back to his car. The best thing for dealing with his rage over what had happened to her was to do something. He pulled away from the curb and headed toward the police station.

He pulled his phone out. A text had come in from one of his fireman friends about a house fire. Let someone else get the story. He needed resolution for Elizabeth, or he wouldn't be able to sleep either.

He dialed the personal number of the detective who would be handling the search at the golf course.

Glenn picked up on the second ring. "Zach."

"Anything?"

"We've searched the grounds and the surrounding woods but we didn't find anyone. There were a lot of people leaving the ball. He could have just gotten in his car and driven off before we had a chance to detain and question people."

He squeezed the phone a little tighter. He really had hoped for an end to all this. "I'll try to talk her into coming in tomorrow to make a statement."

"She can do that. But there is zero evidence," said Glenn.

Zach's stomach tightened. "What happened tonight must be connected with her abduction."

"Maybe, but we need evidence. Did you see the guy?"

"No, he ran off by the time I got to her."

Glenn took a moment to answer. His voice dropped half an octave. "A television reporter like that is used to lots of attention."

Zach gritted his teeth. "She's not like that. She wouldn't make something like this up."

Glenn took a moment to answer. "We'll focus our energy on the previous kidnapping. We have something to work with there. I don't know what tonight was about."

His jaw clenched. He didn't want to get into an argument with his friend. "I just need you to do your job."

"You know we will, but we can't put man hours into investigating an attack with no leads. Bear in mind that I am sure Elizabeth Kramer has some major PTSD going on from the abduction. That kind of thing can mess with your head."

PTSD. There were those letters again. Now he and Elizabeth had that in common. Prayer was the only thing that had kept him from spiraling down to a place where he'd lost all perspective. "She's not safe until this guy is behind bars. That's all I'm saying."

"We are doing everything we can," said Glenn.

Zach hung up. He checked his texts again. Maybe he could still make the fire. A text had come in from Elizabeth.

Someone is in my house.

Elizabeth had changed out of her ruined ball gown when she detected a smell in her bedroom that seemed foreign—a woodsy, damp smell. Her breath caught. Had a man been in her bedroom while she'd been changing in the bathroom?

Her gaze darted around the room. One of her coats had fallen on the floor, and the chair by her makeup table was askew, but it was the lingering odor that made her heart pound. She couldn't take any chances. She grabbed her clutch and slipped into a closet.

Zach was probably not far away. She texted him.

While her heartbeat drummed in her ears, she listened. Had the culprit just been here and left or was he still in the house? The smell was so strong.

She heard noise in her office next door. It could be her cat.

Was she losing her mind? Was she just imagining things? It wasn't a chance she was willing to take.

She thought she heard a door easing open.

She squeezed her eyes shut.

Please, let that be Zach.

She checked her phone again. He hadn't replied to her text. More footsteps. She pressed her back against the closet wall. The clothes shielded her. But if someone wanted to find her, they could.

"Elizabeth." Zach's voice was barely above a whisper.

Relief filled her. She leaned forward and pushed open the door. He hurried toward her from across the room and gathered her in his arms.

How easy it was to fall into his arms. Embarrassed, she pulled free of the embrace and looked up at him. "Did you see him?"

"No, but let's search the house together." He moved toward the bedroom door. "What tipped you off?"

"A smell in my bedroom." The moment she said it, she realized how ridiculous it sounded.

He stared at her a moment too long.

"What are you thinking?" she asked.

"It doesn't sound like the police are actively investigating what happened at the country club." He pressed his lips together. "They just don't have that much to work with, but they are all over the abduction."

So now the police thought she was some kind of unstable nut job crying wolf. "I know someone was in my bedroom." She kept her eyes on the floor as doubt filled her mind.

He touched her hand just above the elbow. "I believe you. Do you have a back door?"

She appreciated the vote of confidence from Zach, but wondered if he had some doubts, too. She led him through her office to the back door. Now she was beginning to wonder if her own fear had made her smell something that wasn't there. She didn't like the way the stalker was able to mess with her mentally even when he wasn't around.

Zach stepped outside. "This door was locked?"

"Both doors were." She leaned to look at the door handle. It didn't look like it had been forced. She let out a heavy sigh. "Nothing."

"Wait a sec." Zach took out a penlight and shone it on the keyhole. "See these scratches? I would say that someone used a lock pick to get it open."

"Or those scratches could have been there from a long time ago."

Zach straightened his back. "If you say someone was in the house, then someone was in your house."

She liked him even more for believing her when she'd started to doubt herself.

"I can't stay alone in the house tonight," she said.

"Is there a friend you can call?"

"Not this late at night."

"You can ride shotgun with me," he said. "I got a text about another fire."

"A news story," she said, remembering the threat her kidnapper had made. "Another fire."

"I won't be the first one on the scene. You'll be safe in my car."

Might as well face her fear. Not having to cover the story would allow her to watch. Maybe her stalker would show up to the fire. Maybe he was the one who had started it. Then again, he must have noticed that she wasn't on the broadcast for the last three nights. She braced herself against the terror that made her legs feel like cooked noodles. "I'll go with you."

As they sped across town, Zach wondered if he'd made the right choice in letting Elizabeth tag along. What other option did he have? He wasn't about to leave her alone again. The police weren't taking her second complaint seriously. She needed someone to be on her side and to keep her safe.

She crossed her arms over her body. "So did you miss getting the scoop on this fire because you came back for me?"

"Course not, Betsy," he said. "Every once in a while you've got to throw the competition a bone or they stop trying, and where's the fun in that?"

"Right." Amusement colored her voice.

As he turned onto a residential street, he saw the cloud of smoke that indicated which house was on fire.

Her back stiffened, and she reached out for the dashboard.

He struggled to say something that would alleviate her fear. "He wouldn't be dumb enough to set a fire twice."

"I hope you're right about that," she said.

Her words had sounded a bit hollow. Both of them had done enough reporting to know that criminals often stuck to a pattern.

Orange-and-black flames shot out from the windows of the two-story house. Police held back the growing crowd while the firefighters worked to control the blaze.

He parked the car away from the lights, so

Elizabeth wouldn't be visible from the street. "Lock the doors if you need to. This won't take more than ten minutes."

"I'll stay here." She held up her phone. "I'm going to send some texts to people who might know if Randy Smith was paroled."

Zach got out of the car. As he ambled toward the scene, he recognized Neil Thompson and the print reporters from the *Chronicle*. Neil spotted Zach and sauntered up to him.

"You're a little off your game, aren't you?"

Zach really wanted to punch Neil. He oozed arrogance anytime the camera wasn't on him. Zach quelled his irritation and squared his shoulders. "I wouldn't say that."

"Saw you earlier at the Waltz." Neil patted his perfect hair. "But you left before I did—it shouldn't have taken you so long to get here. Maybe you're spending a little too much personal time with Ms. Kramer. Or are you just trying to get the interview no one else has been able to get?"

Now he really wanted to hit the guy in his perfect white teeth. "That's not how I operate, Neil. I have something called ethics." Zach walked away before he lost it.

While he was filming the fire, he saw Jim, one of the firemen he knew. Jim had sat down to rest on the truck and gestured him over.

"You're late," he said.

So everyone had noticed. He bit his tongue and tried to sound upbeat. "First time for everything." He angled back toward the fire. "What do you know?"

"No one was at home. Family was on vacation."

"Cause?" Zach studied the scene.

"Not clear. Maybe electrical and maybe…"

"The fire had a little help," Zach said.

"We're still in the prelims of the investigation," said Jim. "We'll know more once our guy can get in there and have a look."

Zach patted Jim on the back. He finished up his story, took some pictures and then stared at the gathering crowd, watching the faces as trepidation crept over him. Was Elizabeth's stalker out there waiting for her to show up? Would he be able to keep her safe?

SIX

Elizabeth jumped when the doorbell rang the next afternoon. Zach. She'd found out that Randy Smith was on parole and lived not far from Badger. The police didn't see talking to Randy as a priority, so she'd decided to take matters into her own hands. She wanted this to be over, to feel like she could take a deep breath again and go back to work without being afraid.

When she'd shared her plan, Zach—who seemed to have appointed himself her bodyguard—insisted that he go along with her. She didn't mind his company, but it bothered her that she couldn't find any record of a Zach Beck having worked for any newspaper in the Baltimore area. Why had he lied?

She opened the door.

Zach was dressed in his usual ripped jeans and T-shirt. The five-o'clock shadow he'd dealt with for the ball was already making a reappearance.

"You ready?"

She nodded. They walked out to his car. The sunlight made the blond highlights in his hair glisten. He had an even, confident stride.

She wanted to believe that Zach was an honest person. Nothing he'd said or done indicated anything different. It touched her that he had given up being first at the fire to come to her rescue.

Still…her reporter instinct wouldn't let her rest until she had a clear answer. But now wasn't the time to ask. They got into the car and drove out of town.

Zach kept his eyes on the road. "How do you want to do this?"

"You mean talking to Randy Smith?"

"The guy did threaten you the last time he saw you in court," he said.

"He lives with his wife, his mom and two kids. I'm hoping he won't try anything with his family there." Even as she said it, she wondered if she was stepping into a dangerous situation.

"Does he know you're coming?"

"I thought it would be better to surprise him." Elizabeth gripped the armrest. The more they talked about this, the more anxious she became.

They reached the outskirts of Badger, and Zach turned onto a country road. "There are two of us, so he's not likely to try anything even if he's alone. I can do the interview if you like."

"I know the questions to ask without being direct to fish out if he's connected to all this," she said. She didn't like that he questioned her professional abilities. Maybe she was still competing with him a little.

"I know you do, Betsy." He gave her shoulder a friendly punch.

She let out a huff of air and shook her head. He had a way of lightening the mood no matter what.

The road clipped by and then wound up one side of the mountain and down the other. A farmhouse with a barn came into view. Zach shifted in his seat. "This is kind of isolated out here."

Tension knotted down her back. "Like I said, the family should be around."

He pulled up to the farmhouse. His shoulder brushed hers as he leaned over and flipped open the glove compartment, retrieving a gun and a box of ammunition rounds.

Her breath hitched. "Really?"

"It was *armed* robbery that he was put away for, right?" He pushed open the cylinder of the revolver and loaded the chamber. "When I was covering the action in A-stan this was standard-issue for reporters."

"Afghanistan? Really, Badger must be a step down, excitement-wise, from covering a war."

It was the first hint he'd given about his past experience, aside from his mention of Baltimore.

She saw the color burning his cheeks just as he turned away and pushed open the door. Apparently he'd revealed more than he'd intended. She could read his body language well enough to know it wasn't the time to press him. What had happened over there? Why was he so secretive?

Zach shoved the gun in his waistband and made his way through a rickety gate to a porch that had an old couch on it. A hound dog came around from the side of house, eyeballing them but not barking.

Zach knocked on the door.

The place looked pretty deserted. A breeze blew across the porch causing the wind chimes to tinkle.

Footsteps pounded from inside the house, and the door swung open. An older woman in a housedress with piercing blue eyes furrowed her forehead. This had to be Randy's mother. "We're looking for Randy Smith," Zach said.

"He's out in the shop." She pointed across the field at the barn. "He wasn't expectin' no customers today."

They thanked the woman and walked away. Elizabeth breathed a sigh of relief that she didn't have to explain who she was. They walked across the field. The knot in her stomach grew tighter. An image of Randy Smith's face distorted with hate when he was in the courtroom flashed through her mind. What were they walking into?

Zach stepped out in front of her. She appreciated his protective instincts, but she didn't want him to think she couldn't handle things herself. Maybe he had been in a war zone, but she had been in plenty of sticky situations, too.

She quickened her pace to catch up with him, her competitive spirit kicking into high gear. "Let me do the talking. I can handle it."

He'd seen her at her weakest that night of the abduction, and then again when she'd nearly drowned. She didn't want him to think she couldn't do her job anymore. An interview was an interview whether you had a personal connection to it or not.

They stepped inside the workshop, which was dusty and poorly lit. At first, she wasn't sure there was even anyone inside. The barn was huge and filled with farm equipment in various stages of disrepair. While her heart pounded against her ribs, she waited for her eyes to adjust to the dimness as she scanned the length of the room.

"Hello," Zach called.

A bald head appeared above the front end of the tractor. Randy Smith. "Yes?"

It was so dim and there was so much distance between them, she was sure he couldn't see who she was. He was a big man. In the courtroom, he'd had a menacing demeanor. She had felt the anger rolling off him. The memory made her shudder.

Even though she was afraid, she'd squared her shoulders and lifted her chin. The best strategy would be to act like she was here for a follow-up interview about his release and then hint about her kidnapping to gauge his emotional reaction.

She took several steps toward him. "I don't know if you remember me or not."

Randy came out from behind the tractor as he wiped his hands on a rag. His face was like carved granite, giving away nothing.

She sensed that Zach was right behind her.

Recognition spread across Randy's face slowly. She steeled herself for the anger, prepared to dash for the door if she had to.

"Yeah." He tossed the rag in a bucket. "I remember you." He stalked toward her.

She planted her feet. "I heard you were released from prison. I was wondering if you would do a follow-up interview."

He reached out his hands toward her just as

a smile spread across his face. He took her into an awkward hug. "This is the lady that saved my life."

He pushed back from the hug, his hands still cupping her shoulders. Face beaming.

Still stunned from his response, she blinked several times unable to form a question. This was not the man she'd seen in the courtroom.

Randy finally let go of her, but continued to stand in front of her, beaming. "Going to jail was the best thing that ever happened to me. Got my life straightened out with the Lord. Got my family back."

Elizabeth relaxed a little. She turned and faced Zach with a what's-going-on-here look on her face. Zach lifted his hands and shook his head.

Randy pointed the wrench at her. "All 'cause you did your job, lady, you and that lawyer."

Zach cleared his throat. "It's a rare day when a lawyer is praised."

She laughed, amazed at how different Randy was. "A lawyer and a reporter lauded in the same sentence—that's even rarer." So Randy was a dead end, but the trip out here had been worth it, to see a changed man. And to hear that her work had something to do with that.

They spent several more minutes visiting with Randy, explaining the real reason they had come before leaving. He had been sympathetic and concerned, but hadn't been able to provide them with any clues as to who might be after her. When they got into the car, Zach unloaded the gun and put it back in the glove compartment.

Her gaze fixed on the gun. She tensed up. Not knowing who Zach really was only added to her discomfort.

Zach pointed at the gun. "Totally unnecessary, right?"

She closed the glove compartment. "Not what I was expecting," she said. "What a turnaround."

"Sometimes we have to be in a really dark place before we realize we need God." The tempo of his words changed from their normal cadence.

She studied him for a long moment. "You sound like you're speaking from experience."

His back stiffened. "You sound like you are in reporter mode, Betsy. I like you better when you're in friend mode."

She shook her head. She really did want to know what dark place had brought him back to God. "I'm just making conversation."

A tension settled into the car as Zach drove on in silence for several miles. Their friendship could only go so deep if he was unwilling to open up a little. Then again, she wasn't about to tell him what had happened her senior year of college. And yet, he hadn't put pressure on her to share. Maybe she wasn't being fair. Their relationship made a lot more sense when they were racing each other to the next story.

Randy's low point in his life had given him faith. When she thought about what had happened in Seattle, she knew she had made the opposite choice. She still went to church, but some part of her had gone numb inside, closed off from God. "Funny how faith works different for different people."

He took his eyes off the road momentarily to glance in her direction. "What are you saying?"

Maybe Zach would understand what she'd been through. "Randy hit rock bottom and rediscovered his relationship with God. But sometimes things happen and they rob us of our faith."

He didn't answer right away. "We always have a choice, how we respond to hard things." Zach's expression changed when he checked the rearview mirror.

Suddenly alert, she craned her neck as fear skittered across her nerves. A truck followed closely behind them. "Where did he come from?" She was guessing that the driver was a man since she couldn't see a face clearly.

"I'm not sure," said Zach.

The route back into Badger was on a winding mountain road too narrow for anyone to pass on safely. The truck edged even closer. Zach sped up. Elizabeth gripped the armrest and gritted her teeth. This was not a safe place to speed.

The first tap on their bumper gave their car a jolt. Elizabeth tensed. Zach kept the car steady and pressed the gas. He hugged a curve. If he went any faster, they'd fly off the road without any help from the other vehicle.

The truck hit them again, this time harder. The back end of Zach's car fishtailed. He overcorrected…and the car careened off the road. Heading down the steep mountain, they bounced over the rough terrain. Elizabeth braced herself as the car flipped and slid to a stop.

She waited for the metal to stop rattling and closed her eyes against the impending doom. She didn't think she was seriously injured—but that didn't mean the danger was over.

Would the man who had run them off the road come down to finish them off?

Every muscle in Zach's body felt like it had been beaten with a hammer. With some effort, he clipped himself out of his seat belt and opened his door. Elizabeth pushed on her door.

"It's dented. I can't get it open." Her forehead looked bruised and there was a trickle of blood on her hand.

"My door opens. Let me pull you through my way. Can you unclip your seat belt?"

She nodded and felt around to free herself.

He'd give one guess as to who the driver of the car was. What was that guy's end game anyway? He seemed to want to torment and frighten Elizabeth in the most intense ways. Or did he mean to kill her?

He pulled her across the upside down driver's seat. He could see that the glove compartment was too smashed for him to get the gun out. He looked down at her.

Her eyes were filled with fear. "Can you see him?" She grabbed hold of his arm.

He steadied her by pressing his palm to her cheek then glanced up the road before shaking his head. There was no one in sight…but just because he didn't see the guy didn't mean he wasn't waiting around.

"My car is toast." He pulled out his phone. "Let's see if we can get some help." No signal.

Elizabeth sat up, gripping her knees. "The mountains block the signal. We need to get to more open ground." Her voice trembled.

He was sure a million questions were running through her mind, as well. Their first priority was to get some help. It would be a long walk back to Randy's place. The best option would be to head down the mountain road until they had a cell phone signal or ran into somebody.

He kneeled beside her. "Is anything broken? Are you okay to walk?"

She nodded. "I think so. I'm just…a little shaken up and my ribs are still hurting."

He rose to his feet and held a hand out for her.

He started to lead them up the mountain to the road, but stopped when he saw a dark truck blocking the path. Adrenaline surged through his body. "Go back. Get down behind my car."

"What?" Elizabeth shook her head.

He lifted her and dragged her back toward the car just as the first gunshot hit the rocks close to where they'd been.

She pressed her back against the wrecked car. "What's he doing?"

"He's not going to let us back up on that road." He scanned the landscape around them. They had to get away. He grabbed her hand and pulled her toward the trees.

Another shot boomed behind them as they entered the forest. Would their attacker come down the mountain and continue to pursue them or did he just not want them on the road?

Zach couldn't take any chances. He sprinted, pumping his legs. Elizabeth kept pace with him. Their feet pounded the forest floor. His heart raged in his chest. He pushed a branch out of the way and kept going. When they'd run for some time without hearing any more gunshots, he stopped. Elizabeth, out of breath, leaned over, resting her hands on her knees.

"Do you think we can go back up there?"

He shook his head. He had no idea what the shooter was after. He'd already tried to abduct Elizabeth twice. Maybe the shooter meant to eliminate Zach and grab her a third time. "It's not a chance I want to take. I say we walk parallel to the road but use the trees for cover. We can head back up to the road in a mile or two once we know we've shaken him."

Aware that the shooter might follow them down, he stuck close to Elizabeth. They walked for at least half an hour. The sky had turned from blue to gray. It would be dark soon.

They came to a stream. Elizabeth kneeled, cupping her hand and scooping up water. She looked at the sky. "I think we should get back up to that road now. Maybe we can catch someone going by."

There weren't that many houses out this way. Traffic would be extremely light. Their chances ~t finding someone were slim—but at least the road would be flatter and easier to walk on. He turned and headed away from the trees back up the rocky incline. Rain sprinkled from the sky. He was glad they both had coats on.

The high-velocity ringing of a rifle shot caused him to yank Elizabeth to the ground. The shooter must have been tracking them all along, waiting for them to emerge. Those shots were clearly aimed at him. Now it was clear that the shooter wanted to get Zach out of the way.

He lifted his head to see if he could spot the shooter in the dusk of evening. The rain continued to drizzle from the sky. Elizabeth pressed in close to him. She might be safer if he pushed her away, since the shooter was aiming for him, but it was clear she needed the reassurance of having him close. Some rocks banged against each other up the hill, but he saw no other movement.

He leaned in and whispered in Elizabeth's ear. "Best head back to the trees."

It was a risk to even stand up. They'd be exposed for at least ten seconds. They both jerked to their feet at the same time and ran.

A shot boomed through the air but it went wide. He could make out the dark shadows of the trees five yards away. He could feel Elizabeth pressing close to him, her rapid footfall ringing in his ears.

The trees enveloped them. But Zach had no way of knowing if the shooter was still on their trail. They pushed deeper into the forest.

He stopped for a moment to listen. The cracking of branches on the forest floor told him the shooter had decided to follow them this time.

Elizabeth must have heard it, too. Before he could warn her, she gasped, turned and kept running. Without any distinct landmarks, it was hard to track where they were going as they ran through the twilight.

The footsteps of their pursuer intensified. He was maybe ten yards behind them. The trees had thinned out. Another few seconds and he'd have a clear shot. Zach willed his legs to work harder. He tugged on Elizabeth's sleeve, pulling her toward some brush. He dove to the ground and she followed.

A moment later, the shooter pounded past them. Some distance away, his footsteps slowed. He returned, retracing his steps.

"Come out, come out where ever you are." His tone was playful and cruel, almost sadistic.

Elizabeth's shoulder touched his. He felt her cringe when the man spoke. The shooter paced a circle around them, hitting the brush with a stick. After a moment, a flashlight flooded the area. Zach's heart skipped a beat.

They had only seconds before they were spotted.

SEVEN

Zach could see their attacker's feet and waited until the man's back was to them before Zach leaped up and pounced. The man, who was twice his size, whirled around and threw him to the ground. Zach hoped that Elizabeth would seize the opportunity to run without being told. He wanted to keep her safe.

Zach recovered and jumped to his feet. Though he was not as muscular as this man, he was quick—and tall enough to have a long reach. He landed several punches before the other guy got in a single blow. Elizabeth was suddenly on top of the assailant, riding his back and wrapping her arm around his neck.

Zach glanced around for the rifle but couldn't see it. The man threw Elizabeth off and then lunged toward her. Zach picked up a branch and landed a blow to the man's head. He toppled to the ground but continued to move. They had only a few seconds head start.

He grabbed Elizabeth's hand and pulled her through the trees. They ran without stopping until the forest thinned and opened up to a wide meadow. The sky had turned almost black. Their steps became more cautious. The rain soaked through their summer jackets and slicked the ground beneath their feet.

He glanced over his shoulder. None of the shadows moved toward them. Only forest noises hit his ears. In the urgency to get away, he'd completely lost track of which way they'd gone.

If they weren't careful, they'd circle back around and end up in the hands of their pursuer.

"Do you think he gave up?" Her voice sounded faint and faraway.

"Doubt it, but I do think we lost him… for now." He pointed toward the edge of the meadow. "Let's rest."

She collapsed on the ground, and he sat down beside her. She tilted her head. "Do we wait for daylight?"

"I don't think that's a good idea." He checked his phone again. Still no signal. The clock on his phone said it was past nine. Staring at the phone reminded him of the map he'd viewed before driving out to Randy Smith's. They'd gone north to reach Smith's farm. If they headed south, they should eventually collide with the road. What he wasn't sure of was if he could avoid their stalker. "I have a little experience with navigating by the stars from when I was in the desert. I think I can get us out of here."

"The desert? When you were covering the war?"

Her voice didn't have the same probing reporter tone to it from before. Or maybe she was just tired. All the same, he felt himself shutting down, not wanting to share about his experiences. In that moment, he realized that his move to Montana hadn't just been to avoid being a news story. It was about avoiding recalling the experience in his mind and heart, as well as in newspaper pages. If no one knew what he'd been through, he didn't have to talk about it or relive it. Maybe he'd been running away from more than just press coverage.

Her voice reached him in the darkness. "Everything okay?"

He was still trying to process the realization. It was why her probing bothered him. He didn't want to feel that terror of nearly dying all over again. Didn't want to smell the stench in the room again the way he would if he described it. "Are you rested?" he said, instead of answering her. "We should get moving."

He could stuff down the memories for now; they had a more pressing threat to contend with.

"Sure, Zach, let's go." Though she couldn't see Zach's face, she could feel him pulling away emotionally. The silence that fell between them as they walked only confirmed that she had touched a nerve. She'd heard pain in his voice.

Why couldn't she just be his friend and turn off the reporter instinct? He had extended her that respect by not demanding to know what had happened to her in college after Neil had mentioned it.

They walked for what seemed like hours though the sky remained dark and the rain stopped. Her stomach growled. She shivered.

She wondered if anyone had driven by and noticed their wrecked car. She doubted anyone in Badger was aware of their absence. Zach worked for himself and since she wasn't scheduled to work, only her cat would be alarmed that she had not come home.

Zach stopped for a moment, turning a half circle.

"Are we lost?" As if her spirits couldn't sink any lower, a new disappointment crept in.

"We're headed in the right direction, but I think that we should pray," he said.

"Pray?" The word sounded foreign on her

tongue. On the outside, it looked like her faith was in tact, but she knew different. She hadn't really prayed for ten years.

"Sometimes it's all you have," he said.

He spoke with conviction as if it was a truth born out of a hard experience. If she had learned anything tonight, it was to hold her tongue and not argue when Zach's voice filled with such intensity.

She couldn't see his expression in the darkness, but she took a step toward him. "Okay then. Let's pray."

"We should have done it hours ago." He grabbed her hands and bowed his head. He prayed for their safety and for them to find something that would lead them back to civilization.

His hands were warm despite the night chill. He squeezed her fingers and then let go. "Now I'm confident that we will find a river or a road or something that will lead us out of here."

She wasn't so sure. She knew more about unanswered prayer than answered prayer. She feared they were walking in a circle. They trudged on for another ten minutes. Zach quickened his pace.

"I hear a river, come on," he said.

She didn't hear it, but she would trust his

senses. He spurred into a jog, and she ran alongside him.

Now she heard it, the rushing of the water. Joy surged through her in spite of her pessimism. Okay, so sometimes God did answer prayer that fast. Yet she'd prayed for justice when Craig had raped her and she'd seen none of it...ever. That had been the start of her fractured faith.

They hurried along the bank, the murmuring roar of the water filling her ears. She could feel the fatigue in her muscles. "Could we rest just for a short time?"

He turned a half circle. "I think that would be okay." He led her to a tree by the river that provided some shelter from the rain.

She collapsed to the ground, and he sat down beside her. The sound of the river washing over rocks surrounded them.

His voice floated on the air. "Are you tired? You can rest your head against my shoulder."

Normally, she would have hesitated but the fatigue got the best of her, and she leaned against the hard muscle of his shoulder. Being close to a man or alone with one always made her uneasy. But she felt comfortable with Zach. Her body relaxed and her eyelids grew heavy. The soft hum of the river lulled her to sleep.

She dozed for less than half an hour and then awoke with a start. Fear shot through her.

Zach patted her shoulder. "It's all right. I've been watching. I haven't seen any sign of him."

She scooted away from him. "You didn't rest?"

"My body rested, but I kept my eyes open. Someone needed to keep watch." His tone darkened. "Someone always needs to keep watch."

He must be referencing something from his time as a war reporter. His comment had opened a door for her to probe deeper, for her to ask questions to uncover who he really was. She chose not to step through that door because that's what a friend would do.

"Come on, we better get moving," he said. He stood up and held out his hand.

She reached for it in the dark, feeling the strength of his fingers as he pulled her up. They walked along the river with the dome of the night sky above them. The rustling roar of water cascading over rocks guided them in the darkness.

Daylight came slowly, turning the sky a soft blue and pink as the sun warmed her face.

He stopped short and pointed. She let out a breath. Up ahead, surrounded by trees on two sides, was a cabin.

"Maybe there will be someone there who can help us," he said.

No smoke furled out the chimney. "Guess we better give it a try."

They raced across the meadow and knocked on the door. No answer. The slide lock on the door was designed to keep bears out, not people.

"I think we should go inside. There might be something that could help us," Zach said. The door swung open, creaking on its hinges. The cabin was empty though it was clear someone was staying there. There was a sleeping bag on a cot and a huge binder.

"Go on in. There might be food or a way to contact someone. We'll leave a note letting the owner know we meant no harm."

Elizabeth stepped inside and wandered around. The binder said National Forest Service on it. Probably a ranger doing research was staying here.

Zach searched the cupboards. "He's got all his food up high in canisters." Zach found a chair and pushed it toward one of the cupboards.

"The ranger is probably out in the forest somewhere gathering data. We could wait. He's got to come back sooner or later," she said.

Zach hesitated in his movement, visibly considering what she was suggesting.

Maybe he was thinking about a less welcome guest showing up. The night time had provided them with a degree of cover. She just couldn't imagine their attacker being able to track them this far. Still, she knew she couldn't let her guard down.

He opened several other canisters before tossing her a package. "Eat up."

She looked down at the protein bar, ripped it open and took a bite. It was hard not to inhale the food considering the empty hole in her stomach. Zach put the canisters away and then dove into his meal.

They both seemed to be eating with a sense of urgency. When they finished, he found a water bottle. He let her have the first few sips while he left a note for the ranger.

"We should at least check the area," she said. "Maybe the ranger's close by."

He glanced out the window and then stepped outside to look around. "There's a dirt road that leads out from here. We can see where that leads."

She scrambled to catch up with him. Fresh tire tracks were embedded in the road. They jogged at a steady pace. She saw the glint of metal through the trees. She hesitated for only a moment, wondering if it was the man who had run them off the road. She angled between the trees where sunlight peeked through. The SUV, which was parked by a river, was clearly marked as a US Forest Service vehicle. She surveyed the river until she spotted a woman in a ranger uniform kneeling by it, filling a container with water. She screwed a lid on the jar, pulled a marker out of a shirt pocket and wrote something on it.

They'd found help. Elizabeth thought she would cry.

The ranger looked up at them and then ambled in their direction, stopping to pick up some other sample containers.

"Boy, are we glad to see you." Elizabeth's voice filled with joy verged on tears. They must both look a little worse for wear.

The ranger's expression didn't give much away. Maybe she'd encountered a few lost people wandering around the forest.

"Our car got run off the road. We've been walking all night," Zach shouted across the river.

The ranger set her water samples into a plastic bin and straightened up, placing her hands on her hips. "I hadn't heard any reports of a vehicle being found."

"The man who ran us off the road took some shots at us," said Elizabeth.

"I suppose you folks will need a ride into town," said the ranger.

Elizabeth's throat went tight. "Yes, we do."

"Let me get across the river, and we'll see what we can do. There's a natural bridge just downstream a ways. I'll be over in few a minutes." She tucked her bin of samples under her arm and trotted downriver, disappearing into a grove of cottonwoods.

When the woman appeared on the other side of the river, Elizabeth felt herself relax for the first time since the car accident.

The ranger got to her SUV, pulled her keys out and unlocked the doors. She offered them a big smile. "I'm Janice, by the way."

Elizabeth slid to the middle of the front seat and Zach got in beside her on the passenger side.

She took in a deep breath. They were on their way home. They were safe…for now.

As Janice's SUV climbed the rugged hill up to the road, Zach couldn't let go of the tension he felt from being chased and nearly killed. Chalk it up to having spent so much time in war zones. He knew that as soon as you relaxed, the guy in front of you or the building you were standing beside got blown to smithereens.

Janice said, "I will make sure the proper authorities looks into what happened to you two. So do you think it was just some guy getting his jollies?"

He felt Elizabeth's body stiffen beside him. Neither of them answered for a long moment.

"I think it was more personal than that," Zach said finally.

Janice seemed to pick up that they weren't ready to talk about what they'd just been through yet. "It happened on National Forest land, but we'll get it coordinated with the sheriff."

The SUV lurched up onto the road. He craned his neck to look out the rear window. No one was behind them.

He'd have to make arrangements to have what was left of his car towed into town. He doubted the police would find any fingerprints on it or much evidence. Maybe some of the paint from the other truck had rubbed off on his at the moment of impact. Not really much to go on.

The road leveled out, and Janice came to a rural gas station that was also a bait-and-tackle shop.

"I've got to fuel up," said Janice. "And get a few things." She got out of the SUV.

"Are you thirsty or hungry?" he asked Elizabeth.

"I could eat a raccoon raw," she said.

Zach chuckled at such a country-bumpkin saying from such a sophisticated woman. He shook his head.

She shrugged and raised her eyebrows. "What?"

"I just didn't expect you to talk like that."

She smiled at him. "I did grow up around here."

"I doubt they have any raccoons, but I'll go see what I can find." He entered the store and looked around. One side of the store was filled with everything the fisherman or hunter might have forgotten, and the other side had mostly junk food and canned goods. Anything would taste good at this point. He grabbed some bottled water and beef jerky.

Janice had come in from filling her gas tank and was chatting with one of the other customers by the fishing supplies.

He placed his merchandise on the counter and pulled out his wallet. The teenage cashier rang him up. When he glanced out the window, a dark-colored truck with tinted windows eased through the gravel lot, moving slowly as though it were looking for something…or someone.

The teenager pushed buttons on the cash register and then took a step back. "I'm sorry, but my computer is frozen. It just takes a second sometimes."

His heart beat faster. He couldn't see the ranger's SUV at all through any of the windows. The dark truck was no longer in view either.

The teenage clerk offered him an apologetic grin and looked at her screen again. "Any second now."

"I'll be right back." He raced outside to check on Elizabeth. The SUV was where they'd left it…but when he yanked open the door, Elizabeth wasn't there. He turned a half circle feeling a rising panic. The truck with the tinted windows was gone, as well.

Janice came out of the store, holding a full grocery bag. "The clerk said you forgot your change." She held it out to him. "Something wrong?"

"It's Elizabeth, she's not in the car." His voice was level despite the brewing thunderstorm inside.

Janice remained calm. "Let's not jump to conclusions. Maybe she just wanted to stretch her legs."

He stared at the surrounding forest. His chest felt like it was in a vise.

"Let's just go have a look around." Janice headed to the far side of the store.

If Elizabeth had just slipped out to stretch her legs, surely she would have stayed close to the car. She knew the danger.

He stalked over toward the bench outside the store. A kid had been sitting there with his dog since they pulled in. Maybe he'd seen something.

"Zach?"

Relief spread through him at the sound of Elizabeth's voice.

"Where did you go?" He tried to sound casual, not wanting to give away how worried the thought of her being harmed had made him.

"The little girls' room. It's not part of the store. It has a separate outside entrance."

He let out a breath. "Yes, of course."

"Is everything okay?"

"Yeah, sure. Everything's fine. Let's get back into town and deal with this," he said.

She studied him for a moment.

Janice came up to them. "Oh, good, Zach was worried that something had happened to you."

"We should probably get going," said Elizabeth, still not taking her eyes off Zach.

She climbed into the car, and he scooted in beside her. Her shoulder pressed against his.

What surprised him was how intense his fear had become when he thought something had happened to her. Yes, he felt a responsibility to protect her. But this was more than that. When he thought something had happened to her, he'd realized just how much he cared about her.

But now was the worst possible time to pursue his feelings. Even if he felt he was ready for a relationship—and he didn't—they couldn't afford to be distracted by romance right now. His panic had been unfounded—this time. But the kidnapper was clearly stalking her, and he seemed to show up when they least expected it. Next time, they might not escape.

EIGHT

Elizabeth's heart raced as she jumped into the driver's side of the KBLK van. She tried to make herself calm down. Her first story since coming back to work was so minor she didn't even need her cameraman, Dale. Small-town news required that you wear more than one hat and today she would set up her own shots. It should be simple, and completely without surprises. *Should* be.

She took in a breath and pressed her back against the seat. Even though fear encroached around her thoughts, it was good to be back. She'd missed working, and appreciated the distraction from her own problems. After starting the van, she hit the blinker and pulled out onto the street.

The story was a fun piece that would probably run at the end of the broadcast for entertainment. A moose had surprised some people with an early morning rampage through a campground. Her boss had probably given her a lightweight story to ease her back into work.

She sped down the highway and turned out onto the frontage road. The campground was a ways out of town. She drove for a half hour before seeing the signs for the campground. As she pulled in, she wondered if her stalker was waiting for her here.

Tension wrapped around her chest as she studied the gathering crowd. The police still had no leads on who had run Zach and her off the road.

Zach stood at the center of a cluster of people. She shook her head. No way would she ever beat him to a story. Whoever he was and wherever he'd come from, he was good at his job.

With Zach, she was learning that maybe it was better not to have her reporter's nose in everything. He'd treated her different since they'd been chased through the forest. She saw the glow of affection in his eyes and it scared her. It was not affection she could return.

Zach must have gotten a loaner car. No other news people had made it yet. Neil Thompson was probably right on her heels. The print people might make it out later in the day.

If she could get the story and leave before

Nosy Neil showed up, she'd be overjoyed. She pushed open the door, feeling just a twinge of fear. It would be pretty hard for her stalker to create this news story. Every step out into the public eye, though, gave her pause and made her anxious. She hated that even if he didn't show up, his threat made her hesitant to do her job.

Before she pulled her gear out of the van, she needed to take in the scene. The moose was long gone, so this story would be about finding the person who could describe what had happened in the most colorful way possible, interspersed with shots of the path of destruction the moose had created.

Zach nodded in her direction. Her heart fluttered when their eyes locked. What was that about? They were still working on being friends instead of competitors.

She scanned the crowd. A man barely out of his teens and wearing a baseball hat lifted his head. Her throat tightened as visions of her abduction bombarded her. She shook off the fear. This kid's build was different than the man who had kidnapped her.

The young man's gaze was downcast as he kicked the dirt with his sandal. He might have a story to tell. He glanced up at her when she approached.

"So you had a little excitement earlier," she said.

He offered her a wide grin. "You're that news lady."

Though she remained composed, her stomach knotted. From now on, when someone recognized her, she would wonder if they were remembering the details of her kidnapping.

Zach had assured her that the public had a short memory, but this was rural Montana, where not that much happened anyway.

"I saw the whole thing. Want to see which way he ran?"

Bingo. She had her interview. "I'd love that." She tilted her head in Zach's direction. "You haven't talked to any other reporter yet?"

The young man shook his head.

She couldn't help the excitement that jolted through her. It still felt good that she'd beat Zach to some part of the story. "Can you tell me your name for the broadcast?"

"Henry Simmons." He held out his hand to her and she shook it. "I'll show you which way he went. Don't you want to film this?"

"I usually scout it first since it's not an unfolding news story." Henry would work well for an on-air interview, but she needed to spend a few minutes with him, so he felt comfortable with her asking him questions before turning the camera on. "Lead the way."

Henry started walking and speaking over his shoulder. "I was getting wood for my morning fire. My campsite is some distance from everyone else's." He tromped toward a grove of trees and disappeared.

She hesitated. The sound of the other campers' chatting faded. Was wandering off with Henry a good idea?

Henry poked his head out from behind a tree. "It's just this way."

This was not the man who had stalked her. But her tormentor hadn't been above getting other people to act for him. Giving the waiter at the country club the note had proven that.

She didn't want to lose her story angle. Even though her heart was racing, she hurried into the grove of trees.

Henry spread his arms out. "This is my campsite."

"Nice, it looks like you have everything you need here." The campsite wasn't the story, but Henry was obviously proud of it. If she wanted to win his confidence, she needed to indulge him a little. "So which way did the moose come from?"

"I'll show you." Henry took off from the campsite deeper into the woods.

Each step into the thick forest caused the tension to ratchet up inside her. Her stomach clenched. She was alone in the forest with a man, and the other people were far away. She struggled to get a deep breath.

Henry pointed to a break in the tree line. "He came charging right through there."

Henry clearly meant her no harm, and yet she couldn't let go of the fear that something bad was about to happen. She cleared her throat. "Okay, why don't you show me which way he went back into the camp?" Back to where the other people were.

Henry wrinkled his forehead. "Are you all right?"

She struggled to find her professional composure. "Yes, I'm fine. Let's get back to the camp." She squared her shoulders even though her stomach was still doing somersaults. Why was she falling apart over nothing?

She hurried back toward the more populated part of the campground. An uproar of screams burst out from the crowd.

Someone yelled, "He's back."

A thunderous crashing from pounding hooves and the breaking of tree branches surrounded her. More cries and screams erupted from the crowd. The moose broke through the trees and charged toward her. She and Henry hit the ground in opposite directions as the animal lumbered past her.

She turned to see the tail end of the moose disappear into some trees. Her heart pounded. Footage of the moose would be beyond perfect for this story. She didn't have her news camera but she had her phone.

She jumped to her feet and ran toward where the moose had gone. Adrenaline charged through her. This was what she loved.

"Careful, they're mean." Henry's words pummeled her back.

Her focus was only on getting the shots she needed. She sprinted into an open meadow where the moose had slowed its pace. It snorted and jerked its head. She pulled her phone out of her pocket and clicked to the video camera.

The moose trotted forward as she lined up the shot. Keeping the moose in the frame, she sidestepped while holding the phone steady.

"Beautiful."

The moose stopped and turned in her direction. He snorted and lowered his head, giving her what seemed to be a challenging look. She kept filming. Arms wrapped around her and pulled her to one side. Zach.

She couldn't hide her ire. "You messed up my footage."

The moose stopped short of charging her and disappeared into the trees.

Zach grabbed her arms. His face was close to hers. "What were you thinking? He could have trampled you."

His anger scared her—and that made her annoyed with herself, causing her to snap at him.

"I was thinking I was getting the shot no one else had." She pulled away from him. "That's what I was thinking."

"You could've died," Zach said.

The rest of the crowd, including Neil Thompson and his cameraman, emerged from the trees.

"I appreciate everything you've done for me, Zach. But don't interfere with my work." She spoke just above a whisper, not wanting the crowd to know they'd been fighting.

She whirled around and walked away from him, rubbing her arms where he'd grabbed her. She stomped past Neil.

"Did you get footage of the moose?"

Feeling triumphant, she held up her phone. "The one and only." Elizabeth hurried through the remainder of her work. She set up her camera, did her intro, interviewed Henry and took a few shots of the torn tents and scattered dishes the moose had left in the wake of his escapade.

She spotted Zach several times as he finished up his story. She knew he'd grabbed her to protect her, but it still had brought back a ten-year-old fear and the memory of Craig Miller squeezing her arm so hard it bruised. She put her camera gear back in the van.

What bothered her even more was that the stalker had nothing to do with this news story and yet his threat affected her emotionally and made it hard for her to do her job.

She was the first of the news people to finish up and get her gear loaded. Neil was still wandering around doing interviews. Total overkill. He'd have miles of footage. The producer would have to decide what was useful. Neil wasn't the brightest light in the room. She wondered how he had managed to dig up the information about what had happened to her in college.

She pulled out onto the winding road. Her van whizzed past forest and steep embankments that led down to the river. She'd driven for about five minutes when she noticed the black truck following closely behind her. Her heart fluttered. She sped up. The truck remained close to her bumper. One bump and he could run her off the steep road.

* * *

Zach packed up his gear and jumped into the car he'd gotten for cheap, mentally berating himself for messing up. He'd wanted to be more of a support to Elizabeth with her first story since the assault. Instead, he'd interfered and made her mad.

When he'd seen the moose charging in her direction, the instinct to protect had kicked into high gear. Would he have done the same thing if it had been any other reporter in the same situation? Probably not. His affection for her made him impulsive.

He turned his car toward the country road. His intent wasn't to mess up her footage. The truth was he cared about her, maybe as more than a friend. But any affection he had for her came up against how guarded she was. Friends would be the most he could hope for.

He increased his speed down the country road headed toward the winding mountain that would lead him back into town. Elizabeth's default position for running away from emotion seemed to be to throw herself into her work. He wished he understood why.

His phone pinged indicating he had a text. He glanced over at it on console where it was propped up. The message was from Elizabeth.

Someone is following me.

Adrenaline shot through him as he gripped the wheel. He pressed on the accelerator.

Unless she'd been headed to another story, she had to be on the same road as him. He'd watched her pull out. She had maybe a five-minute head start on him.

He hugged a corner, catching a glimpse of the steep, rocky embankment. Once he was free of the curve, he increased his speed and prayed that he wouldn't reach Elizabeth too late.

NINE

Elizabeth snuck another look into her rearview mirror. The black truck remained glued to her bumper but still hadn't made the move to pass her or run her off the road.

Her heart pounded and her hands were sweaty where she held on to the steering wheel. The news van didn't have a back window. Her view of the truck was limited to the side mirror.

The road straightened, and she increased her speed. She took in a breath to calm her rattled nerves. The truck kept pace with her.

She went even faster as panic roiled through her.

Stay calm.

No matter what she did, she couldn't shake the truck.

The curve came up suddenly, and she fought to compensate. She lifted her foot off the accelerator and swung the van into the other lane. But it wasn't enough.

The accident seemed to happen in slow motion. The van became airborne, slammed into the rocky embankment and rolled down the hill.

Her world clattered and shook. Elizabeth felt as though she'd had the wind knocked out of her. She opened her eyes to peer through a broken windshield. Water rushed over her. She lifted her head so she could breathe.

The van was upside down in a river. She strained her neck to keep it above water. She tried to sit up, but couldn't. She couldn't move one of her arms.

She heard the sound of feet swishing through the water, approaching the van, but her vision was limited. Her neck hurt from the effort of holding her head up.

"Help me." She fumbled around for the seat belt with her free hand but couldn't reach it.

Whoever was moving through the water drew closer. She turned her head as far as she could. She could see boots, nothing else. The man stood in front of the van window for a long time.

She was trapped. If this was her stalker, he could kill her if he wanted to.

The broken glass of the van window distorted her view of his black rubber boots. Her heart pounded. She fought harder to free herself from the seat belt. He stood there, not moving and not speaking for what felt like a day.

The longer he lingered, the more terrified she became.

Finally, he turned and walked away. She listened to the sound of his feet swishing through the water. A few minutes later, she heard a truck start up. Why hadn't he killed her or kidnapped her when he had the chance?

How long could she wait here holding her head above water before she tired? She didn't think she'd be able to last long, not with the blow to her head from the crash that made it hard to even hold her eyes open. Would Zach be able to find her in time?

From the high point on the mountain, Zach was able to see sections of the winding road below him. He'd seen a black truck, but not the KBLK news van. He pressed on the accelerator, pushing the car to its limit on the narrow road.

He caught a glinting flash in his peripheral vision as he whizzed by where the river came close to the road. He pulled out on the first shoulder he saw, hit the brakes and jumped out of the car. He sprinted back to where morning sun had reflected off metal in the river.

His heart seized. The news van was upside down in the river. He raced down the rocky incline and splashed through the water. He kneeled beside the broken window of the van. Though shadows covered the interior, he could make out Elizabeth's head half covered in water.

His throat went tight.

Her eyes were closed, and she wasn't moving.

He reached in and lifted her lifeless head.

Oh, dear God, no.

He pulled a pocketknife out of the sheath on his belt and cut her free of the seat belt. She was like a rag doll in his hands as he dragged her free of the van, lifted her into his arms and carried her to a sandy spot by the river.

His fingers touched the side of her neck. Her pulse pressed back against his fingers, but she wasn't breathing. He pushed on her stomach just below the rib cage, counting out the rhythm, careful not to press into her bruised ribs. Then he tilted her neck and placed his lips on hers to breathe into her mouth.

His vision blurred as a flashback invaded his awareness, remembering dropping his gear and racing toward an injured soldier lying in the desert sand. He'd tried to revive the man but the soldier had died in Zach's arms beneath the blistering sun.

He pushed past the agony the memory brought

with it and focused on Elizabeth's beautiful face. Again, he went through the CPR steps. Praying with each push below her rib cage and then sealing his lips over hers.

Finally, blessedly, she sputtered and coughed up water. Her eyes grew wide and then she wrapped her arms around him and wept.

"I thought…I thought I was…"

He held her close and stroked her wet hair. "It's all right. Everything's going to be okay."

She held on to him tighter and sobbed.

He kept his arms around her until the crying subsided. She pulled away, wiping the tears off her face. She bent her head and looked away, maybe embarrassed over the intense display of emotion.

"Sorry, guess I lost it," she said, still not making eye contact.

He touched her shoulder lightly. "Anybody would have." He shifted so he was sitting cross-legged.

She folded her arms over her body. She was soaking wet. He'd managed to stay dry except for his shoes and the lower half of his pants. He pulled his coat off and placed it on her shoulders.

She drew it to her neck, eyes filled with warm gratitude. "Thank you."

A car stopped on the road above them. She tilted her head. "Oh, great, it's Neil Thompson."

Zach glanced up to see a cameraman already filming the news van. "Come on, let's get you out of here. We can make arrangements for the van to be towed." He held an arm out for her.

She was still visibly shaken from her near-death experience, and Neil showing up only seemed to agitate her more.

She stumbled. He wrapped an arm around her waist and helped her up the rocky incline. Neil stomped toward them, microphone in hand, and gestured for his cameraman to film her.

She held up her hand. "I'm not talking to you."

"I'm thinking of doing a feature piece on accident-prone news reporters," said Neil.

"Shut it, Neil." Zach could feel his anger simmering as he escorted Elizabeth toward his car.

"Just one statement." Neil scurried behind them.

Zach opened the door for Elizabeth and hurried around to the driver's side. Neil gave up and returned to his news van.

Zach pulled off the shoulder and headed down the road.

Elizabeth craned her neck. "When is he going to give up?"

"When he overtakes you in the ratings, so…

probably never. He just doesn't have the skills you have, so he has to be a slimeball."

She slipped her arms through his coat. "My boss isn't going to be happy about that news van."

"So that truck ran you off the road?"

She shook her head. "That's just the thing—the truck didn't have to. I panicked and didn't use good judgment as soon as I saw him behind me. It's like he's inside my head. I almost couldn't do that stupid moose story because of what he said and the things he's done."

"Boy, if someone wanted to destroy your career, this would be the way to do it," Zach said.

She lifted her head. "Stop the car. Pull over."

"What is it?"

Neil's news car pulled in beside her.

She pushed open the door and rushed toward Neil. Zach got out of the car, curious as to what realization had compelled her to make him stop. He was a little fearful that she might just punch Neil Thompson's perfect face.

Neil stood by his car. "Did you change your mind?"

"How did you know about what happened to me in college?" She blasted Neil with the question.

Neil smiled his perfect-teeth grin. "I did my research."

Zach drew a little closer. Elizabeth tilted her head to one side and narrowed her eyes as though she didn't believe Neil.

Neil raised his hands. "All right. I got a tip and then I did my research."

"You don't know the source?"

He shook his head. "It was anonymous." He crossed his arms. "So I gave you something. How about we do a little feature on your accident?"

"Yes, because that would make me look so professional." She turned on her heel and headed back to the car. Zach followed her.

He pulled back out on the road and waited for her to explain. Neil remained behind them but followed at a safe distance.

Finally, she spoke. "That thing you said about someone wanting to destroy my career made me think."

"You think Neil has something to do with this?"

"Maybe. I'm not sure if he's helping my attacker or if my attacker is helping him. Or if it's all just a coincidence. But everything that has happened is making it hard for me to do my job." She shook her head. "I don't get this stalker. He had a chance to either kidnap or kill me there in the river and he did neither. Instead, he just made me really afraid."

The car rumbled down the road as a tense silence settled between them. She stared at her hand, turning it back and forth. She must be thinking deeply.

"I wonder if Neil really did do the research to find out about Seattle," she said.

Zach didn't know how to respond. He'd picked up on the intensity behind each word when she spoke about college. He certainly hadn't come across any scandal about her and he was pretty sure he was a better researcher than Neil.

After a long moment, she said, "I suppose you'd like to know what Neil was talking about?"

"Only if you want to tell me."

She laced her hands together and rested her lips against them. "If we can find a place to pull the car over—"

"I think there is a picnic area at the bottom of the mountain," he said.

He drove around the curve and pulled out to an area that overlooked the river.

He waited for her to speak first.

She twisted a strand of her red hair and spoke without looking at him. "I was date-raped my senior year of college by a man named Craig Miller. He's a lawyer in Seattle now. He never went to jail. The case never even went to trial."

The information barely sank in before he felt his rage rise up against the man who had done such a thing to her. Now he understood why she was so guarded around him.

"I already had a part-time reporter job with a news station. They kept it quiet, but the college newspaper covered it extensively. My name got leaked." She turned slightly away from him. "I needed a fresh start, and a little while later, my dad got sick. It seemed like a good time to come home."

He touched her shoulder lightly. "I'm so sorry."

She didn't pull away from his touch. Instead, she placed her hand on his for a moment. She rubbed the armrest with the other hand and looked off in the distance. When she spoke again, her voice had the reporter tone that he knew she used to help her distance herself emotionally from what she was saying.

"That kind of information wouldn't ruin me as a reporter, but I wasn't comfortable having it out there while I was in the public eye for work. Just like with the assault and the kidnapping, it makes me wonder if people are thinking of that while I'm interviewing them."

"That would be a pretty normal response." He was speaking from experience.

Neil Thompson's car slowed as it went by but didn't stop.

"Guess he's given up for the day," she said.

"Seems like a lot of trouble to destroy someone's career," he said. "I just don't think Neil is smart enough to pull something like this off."

"Like I said, maybe he had help. Or maybe he's telling the truth about the tip being anonymous, and someone's just using him as a tool. It wasn't Neil who grabbed me at the fire or the country club." She rested her head in her hands. "I need to get back to the station and face the music about the news van. Not exactly a great first day back."

He patted her back. "The good news is it can only get better." He turned the key in the ignition. "Come on, intrepid reporter. You can do this."

Her eyes rested on him for a moment, and he thought he detected affection there. Now he understood why part of her was so walled off. A friendship might be the most he could hope for.

She had shared her darkest secret with him. He wasn't sure if he was ready to share his.

TEN

Tension coiled around Elizabeth's throat and shot down into her chest. This story was big, a hostage situation at a ranch. A grown son had barricaded his parents, his younger sister and his wife in the house.

Up to this point, she'd been doing the fluff pieces since her return. After four days of work, her boss had confidence in her that she could handle this big story. Now she just had to believe in herself. She reached out for the dashboard as Dale rounded a curve on the dirt road.

Her cameraman glanced over at her. "What do you know about these people?"

She looked at the notes she'd scribbled when the call had come in. There was not much information. "I recognize the last name. They've had a ranch out here for generations."

"Wonder what made the kid go bonkers."

"It's my job as a reporter to find out," she said. They rounded the corner, and the ranch house came into view. The place was surrounded by police cars. Members of the SWAT team were strategically placed around the house. She saw a sniper on the barn roof.

Sweat formed on her forehead as she curled her hand into a tight fist.

Dale pushed open the van door. "I'll get some opening shots. You gather the information you need for your stand-up."

She squeezed her eyes shut and opened them several times.

Help me, Lord. Help me get through this.

"You all right?" Dale spoke with fatherly concern.

She lifted her chin. "Yes, I'm just taking a breath and coming up with a plan."

That was the most sincere prayer she'd prayed since being lost in the forest with Zach. She wasn't sure why it had felt so natural to turn to God now after so many years of turning away from him—but it *had* felt natural, whether she could explain it or not.

She pushed open the door and stepped out into the summer night. She took in the scene, searching for an officer who might be open to talking to her. Of course Zach was here already. He'd shown up to a lot of her fluff pieces over the past week. Stories he normally wouldn't cover. She wondered if maybe he'd asked her producer to let him know when she was headed out to a story. She wasn't sure how she felt about his protectiveness. Yes, she was afraid every time she went to cover breaking news. But she needed to be strong and professional. As much as she liked his company, having a babysitter worked against her.

Zach made his way toward her.

"I still can't beat you to a story, Mr. Beck," she said.

He shrugged. "You're always the second one." He turned back toward the house and then looked at her. "Here's what I know. After the first phone call where the guy let police know he was going to kill everyone in the house, he broke off communication. The guy's name is Tyler Kinkaid."

She looked at the house. The shades were pulled on all but one window.

Zach kept talking. "They don't know which room of the house he's in. They've seen movement on the second floor."

Feeling a little miffed, she planted her feet. "I could have gotten that information myself. That's my job."

"I'm sorry. I know you could have. I just wanted to help." Hurt tinged his words.

"Zach, I appreciate it, but I have to show that I'm able to do my own reporting."

He nodded and swung his arm in an arc. "Go forth and report."

Was her ire about his over protectiveness or because he knew her secret? She'd closed that door so tightly. Opening it made her afraid as shame rose to the surface. Did he think less of her?

Both of them noticed a police officer making his way over to the chief.

They ran to be within earshot of the exchange. Though she could not pick up the whole of the conversation, she gathered that they had some background on the hostage taker. She heard the phrase *no history of mental illness* and something about a tour of duty.

"He's a vet." Zach's tone was full of emotion, but Elizabeth wasn't sure what the emotion was. Fear? Trepidation? Empathy?

Clearly upset, Zach stalked off, stopping to talk to one of the officers who stood behind the open door of his police car with his gun drawn.

Part of the SWAT team disappeared around the other side of the house. Something seemed to have shifted as far as what was going on. Had they figured out where the hostages were in the house? Maybe Tyler Kinkaid had decided to talk to them.

She didn't see Zach anywhere.

Dale came up to her while she was still looking around for Zach. "Things look pretty tense," Dale said. "Probably no chance for an interview until it's over."

"I have enough prelim info for a live feed. I'm sure they'll want to cut into regular programming. Let's get ready for that."

While Dale placed the camera on the tripod, she wandered behind the line the police had set up to keep reporters from being interfering. Still no sign of Zach. She studied the ranch house, seeing shadows moving around the outside. Her breath caught.

Zach raced from one bush to another straight toward the house where the hostages were being held by an armed man bent on killing them.

Zach had overheard the order that if either of the snipers got a clean shot at Tyler, they were to take it. He couldn't stand the thought of it. While he didn't know what had brought Tyler to the point of holding his family hostage, he knew what men like Tyler had been through and that the former soldier didn't deserve to die here today.

Zach crouched low by the wall of the house until he found an open window. He slipped into a dark, silent basement. He could hear no footsteps above him. The SWAT team hadn't entered the house yet.

He felt along the wall and found his way to the stairs, keeping his ear tuned for any sound above him. By the time he made it to the top stair, adrenaline raged through his body. His heartbeat drummed in his ears. He entered a dark kitchen.

The SWAT team wouldn't want to risk the lives of the hostages. They'd be patient and wait for a moment when they could incapacitate or kill Tyler without harming anyone else. Staying low, he moved along the kitchen island. He detected footsteps, light and fast.

He raised his head. A girl of about twelve or thirteen opened several cupboards and pulled out plastic containers, which she dropped twice. She was clearly agitated. She found a container with a lid and filled it with water.

When she turned around toward the island, he stood up.

He held up his hand and spoke in the softest voice he could manage. "I'm here to save your brother's life."

A look of fear crossed her face as though she were trying to process what he'd said. She raised her voice. "How do I know that's true? Nobody has cared about him since he got back."

He touched his fingers to his lips. "Quiet. You have to be quiet."

Her voice trembled. "He's not a bad person."

"I know. I used to work with soldiers like him."

She shook her head.

"I was a reporter in the Middle East. I've been around these guys."

That news seemed to make her want to cooperate. Her body relaxed. "He's acting crazy. He thinks Mom and Dad are trying to hurt him."

"I understand what he's going through. We don't have much time. There are police outside who will kill your brother if they get a chance. Can you take me to him? I want to help him."

"I'm the only one he trusts," she said. "If I bring you in, he's going to go all crazy and blame me."

"What's your name?"

"Cassie. He's only twenty-two. He's always been a good brother."

He pointed to the water jug. "Did he ask you to bring water up to him?"

She nodded.

"You do that. I'll be behind you. It doesn't have to look like you led me to him. Cassie, we need to hurry before someone gets hurt."

Cassie picked up the water jug and raced toward the stairs. She led him up several flights to an attic. She entered the room while he pressed against the wall by the door.

"Tyler, I have the water you asked for." Cassie's voice trembled.

"What have you been doing, Cassie? What took you so long?" Tyler's words dripped with suspicion.

While still pressed against the wall, Zach eased toward a window and lifted the shade. The SWAT team was moving into the house. They'd go through each floor until they found the hostages.

Cassie sounded like she was about to fall apart. "I wasn't doing anything. Please, I got you the water like you asked. I came back."

Zach tensed. It would take the SWAT team only minutes to clear each floor. He didn't have much time.

He heard stomping and then Tyler yelling. "I just don't get you."

The voice of an older woman said something Zach couldn't understand.

"How long have you wanted me dead?" Tyler shouted.

A different male voice responded. "Son, we've never wanted you dead."

More stomping.

Zach eased toward the door and stared through the slit between the door and the frame.

Three rifles leaned against a wall. Tyler paced the floor, swinging a handgun wildly. Two older people sat on the floor back-to-back and tied up. A young woman sat in a corner with her hands bound. Only Cassie and Tyler were free, and Cassie was cowering in a corner.

Zach steeled himself and slipped into the room. Tyler swung around, pointing the gun at him. His eyes glazed, teeth showing.

Zach put up both his hands in a surrender gesture. Though his heart pounded inside his chest, his voice remained level.

"I'm not armed. There are men coming with guns. They will kill you. You need to put the gun down."

Tyler's finger slipped inside the trigger. "I know you. You've come to hurt me."

"No. Please, I know soldiers like you. I worked as a reporter in Syria and A-stan. I know what you've been through."

Tyler lifted the gun so it was pointed at the ceiling. "You don't know."

Cassie's voice was barely above a whisper. "I think he's telling the truth."

Tyler's posture softened for a moment. Then he pointed the gun at his parents.

Zach rushed to draw Tyler's attention back to him. "When I was overseas, I saw men like you every day. Good men. Men who volunteered to serve their country." Zach took a step closer. "I'm grateful for your service. We all are. And we know it's been hard on you, that you've had trouble since you got back. But your family wants to help. *I* want to help. Please. Let us help you."

Cassie cried out. "Tyler, please."

The sound of men moving up the stairs landed on Zach's eardrum.

Tyler's whole demeanor changed. He seemed to crumple and shrink. "Oh, little sister." Tyler let the gun fall to the floor. Cassie rushed over to him and the siblings whispered back and forth, too low for Zach to hear.

Zach yelled down the stairs. "Can you stand down? I think he'll surrender."

One of the SWAT team members stepped from the shadows holding a high-powered rifle. "And you are?"

Cassie came to Zach's side. "He says he'll come out, but he wants you to go with him."

Zach nodded. "I can do that." He yelled down the stairs. "He's not armed, and he's ready to surrender. I'm bringing him down. It would probably be a good thing if he didn't see you and your guns."

When Zach leaned over the stairs again, the men were gone.

Zach turned his attention back to Tyler, who

had collapsed to his knees and was sobbing, holding his hands over his face. Cassie kneeled beside him, rubbing his back.

"Soldier, if you're ready, I'll escort you out and put you into police custody. I'll let them know that nothing bad happened here tonight. I'm sure your family will back you up in that." Tyler's mom, dad and wife all nodded. Zach would see to it that Tyler got the psychological help he needed, too. Even if the money had to come out of his own pocket.

Tyler rose to his feet, wiped his eyes and squared his shoulders.

"I'll stay right here with you all the way," Zach said.

Cassie gave her brother a hug before he fell in beside Zach. They made their way down two flights of stairs and out into the night. Though he knew they were watching closely, the SWAT team stayed out of sight. He could only imagine the frantic messages being communicated to the snipers and the rest of law enforcement. He suspected once they'd left the house, the team would move straight up to the attic to help the hostages.

When they stepped outside, floodlights caused Tyler to take a step back. He groaned and shielded his face. Zach touched his arm just above the elbow. "Do you want them to turn off the lights?"

Tyler's voice filled with agony. "Yes, please. It's so bright."

A sliver of a memory played out before Zach's eyes. When he was held captive, he'd spent time staring at bright lights while men with brutal voices paced the room in the shadows. The images made him nauseous.

The police chief yelled from the darkness. "What's going on?"

Zach took in the scene in front of him. He was here in Montana. He was safe. "Can you kill the lights, please?" Yet he could not let go of the fear the memory brought to the surface. Fear he'd stuffed away in a dark corner of his mind for a long time.

The lights popped off one by one. A small flashlight flickered on behind one of the police cars.

Tyler stiffened beside him. Zach said, "I'll walk you all the way over there. Police Chief Rains is a good guy."

They made their way across the grass. Zach glanced up. The two snipers were still in place, ready to pull the trigger if anything went wrong.

"Listen to me, soldier. It's very important that we stay calm. Do you understand?"

"Sure, I see the shooters on the barn, too," said Tyler. Once a soldier, always a soldier.

His own stomach felt like it had a tornado whirling through it.

The police chief stepped out from behind the car. He waited for Tyler to move toward him.

The police chief's voice filled with kindness. "Son, you understand why we have to take you in."

Tyler nodded. He turned to face Zach. "Thanks, man, I think you saved my life tonight."

"I'm honored that you let me help. Godspeed, soldier." Zach cupped Tyler's shoulder and watched as he was led away.

Elizabeth was suddenly beside Zach, gripping his elbow and ushering him away. "My turn to help you."

He stared over his shoulder at the slew of reporters headed in their direction.

"The van is right over here. Dale will catch a ride with someone else." She'd been strategic about where she parked for a quick getaway. "The local stations are tapping into national feeds. Your story is going to blow up, nationwide."

He hopped in the passenger seat. She pressed the accelerator before he'd even buckled up. His stomach still felt like it was full of rocks. He stared at the ceiling as memories of his own captivity bombarded him. Memories he could no longer push down.

She drove down the dark road. "My dad had a cabin. No one would think to look for you there."

He couldn't respond. All the images he'd locked away and the emotions that went with the memories assaulted him.

Elizabeth seemed to understand that he wasn't in a place where he could talk. She kept driving deeper into the forest.

If the national news teams had picked up the story, it would only be a matter of time before someone connected the dots and realized he was Zachery Tan Creti, war correspondent from Baltimore, former terrorist captive. He hadn't buried his identity that deep.

It would be better if Elizabeth heard the story from him. She deserved that courtesy.

"Doesn't look like anyone is following us," she said. "I took a bunch of side roads."

"Can you pull over?"

"Sure." She stopped the van.

He got out, ran to the side of the road and threw up several times. He could not hide from the memories any longer. He heard footsteps, and she placed a hand on his back.

"Come on. Let's get you up to that cabin."

She didn't pressure him for explanations. As he heard the compassion in her voice, he was suddenly very grateful to have her as a friend.

Elizabeth awoke in the cabin early and got the generator working. She crept past the couch, where Zach still slept beneath a plain blanket. He hadn't said anything once they'd arrived at the cabin late in the night. She fumbled in the kitchen to find the coffee. It had been months since she'd come up here.

She put the coffee in her father's old percolator, and the room filled with the aroma of the grounds brewing.

As she watched Zach sleep, she wondered where a man found the kind of courage he'd shown. He'd risked his life to save the ex-soldier. And all the while, he seemed to be wrestling with something even deeper than the events of last night.

There was no bacon and eggs to cook, only some granola bars. Not much of a breakfast. She set them on the counter and poured herself a cup of coffee.

Zach stirred awake. "What a great smell."

She turned away embarrassed that she'd been caught staring at him. "Would you like some?"

She poured him a cup and handed it to him. He took it and rose to his feet, staring out the window.

"Sorry, about last night. On the road there."

"I think anybody would have had that kind of a response given what you did," she said.

He shook his head. "It wasn't about that. It's just seeing that kid all messed up like he was…" He paced in front of the window and then collapsed on a chair. "It brought back some memories."

"The war?"

"More than that." He ran his hands through his hair. "I don't know why this is so hard to say—you'd find out soon enough whether I told you or not. I'm sure the footage is going to be all over the news when we get back to town." He paced.

She shook her head. "What are you talking about?"

"I was held hostage in Syria. They killed two of my colleagues. Last night made me relive the whole thing. It just brought everything up." He turned away from her again. "Beck isn't my real last name." He made momentary eye contact with her as if he was gauging her reaction.

Shock spread through her. It must have been reflected on her face because he seemed to crumple in front of her. She was having a hard time absorbing everything he was saying. She really didn't know him at all. "So you're not who you said you were?"

"I'm exactly who I've said I am. I'm a journalist. I can play a decent game of basketball. I like calling people by nicknames. I used to live in Baltimore. I covered the war. All of that is true. The only lie was my last name, and I only lied about that because I came to Montana to get away from everything, including being hounded by reporters. Guess I was running instead of working through it. But the memories followed me here." He stomped toward the door. "I'm so sorry for the deception." He disappeared outside.

She let out a breath. She'd seen the footage from those news stories of different reporters who had been beheaded. She remembered the stories on Zach himself, though she thought his hair had been a different color back then—he must have dyed it. She could not imagine what he must have been through. Her heart filled with empathy and she raced after him.

When she stepped out on the porch, she saw no sign of him. He could have gone in several directions. She called his name. She ran a short distance on one path. Not seeing him, she sprinted back to the cabin and chose another trail.

She found him standing at the edge of a drop-off staring out at the scenery.

She ran up to him and touched his shoulder lightly. "I understand why you did what you did."

He turned, blue-gray eyes flashing. "Do you?"

She nodded. "I've experienced the press hounding after the assault, and what you went through was much more traumatic."

"Both of us have been through something few people experience," he said. "I never meant to deceive you."

There was so much about him she was only beginning to understand. Yes, there had been deception. But his courage only hours earlier and in the face of death in the Middle East was what stood out to her. "It's all right."

Relief spread across his face. His gaze rested on her. She felt herself being magnetically pulled toward him. He gathered her into his arms. His lips found hers, and she yielded, drawing closer to him as warmth spread over her.

Ten years. It had been ten years since she'd kissed anyone.

Fear encroached. She pulled away, bombarded with her own memories of violence.

"I'm so sorry. I can't do this. I'm happy being your friend." It was her turn to run away. She hurried back to the cabin and shut the door.

Tears streamed down her face as she placed a hand over her mouth. Grief and pain over what had been stolen from her that night ten years ago washed through her. She'd been running, too, just as Zach had—staying busy with work so she didn't have to think about that terrible night.

She went into the bedroom and closed the door. Wiping the tears from her eyes, she realized how conflicted she felt. She did want to be more than friends with Zach. She'd never known anyone like him. The walls were just too high and the fear too great.

She slumped down on the bed. She uttered the sentence she had not let herself think for ten years.

"God, why did You let this happen?"

Now she had met someone that she maybe could have a life with and because of Craig Miller, she couldn't let a wonderful man like Zach in. Her sobbing subsided, and she lay down on the bed. "God, You could have kept me safe that night and You didn't. Why?" She pulled the covers up around her. Even uttering the question seemed to break something loose inside her. She found herself talking to God, telling Him everything she felt, the sorrow and the anger.

She heard the outside door open. Zach must be coming inside. Part of her wanted to go to him and talk. And then she half hoped he would open the door and come in and hold her.

She listened to him shuffling around. Slowly, the emotional exhaustion overtook her when she realized he wasn't going to come in to her, and she didn't have the courage to go out to him.

She closed her eyes. At least something had shifted between her and God.

She opened her eyes and stared at the ceiling. They couldn't hide out in this cabin forever. It wouldn't be safe. The man who wanted to harm her was still out there...waiting and watching. And he seemed to have a knack for finding her.

ELEVEN

Zach drew back the curtain on his second story apartment. The news crews were still outside as they had been for the last three days. When he'd been released in Syria and come back stateside, he'd done a news conference outside his sister's house thinking that would placate the press's hunger, but it had only made them want more juicy details. As though the trauma of his life was a movie.

This time he wasn't going take the bait. He had no statement to make about why he'd stepped in to save Tyler or why he'd come to Montana under a different name. They could not begin to understand. They didn't *want* to understand. They wanted salacious details and flashy headlines.

His phone beeped, indicating he had a text. He picked it up. Elizabeth. They hadn't spoken of the kiss when they left the cabin together. He knew he'd been out of line the second she'd pulled away. He'd been thinking about what he wanted, not what she needed. She'd been so understanding about his deception. It had only increased the bond he felt for her.

He read her text.

I'm here to help you escape the press because you did that for me. I'll be in the alley in five minutes. Only one reporter is camped out at the back of the building. I did my recon.

He shook his head. She was a good friend. Maybe this was her way of making things less awkward between them. He hurried down the stairs and spotted the reporter right away. He pressed against the wall and waited for the man to turn his back before he sprinted into the alley.

Elizabeth sat in her little compact car. The engine was still running when he jumped into the passenger seat.

"You made it." She gave him a look he couldn't quite decode. She was smiling but there was something behind her eyes. Fear maybe. Uncertainty?

How could he ever get to the place where she felt safe around him again? He'd destroyed so much with one kiss.

"Where are we going?"

She hit her blinker as she turned out onto the street. "Are you hungry? You probably haven't been able to go to the store."

"I've been living on energy drinks and canned goods."

"Ick. Let's go get you some decent food," she said.

"I can't go out in public."

"I have food at my house."

He caught of flash of motion in the side view mirror. "There's always one sharp reporter in the bunch. Looks like we're being followed."

"I hope it's a reporter." Her voice trembled.

He felt like a heel for having forgotten for a moment that her terror was driven by something much worse than a rabid journalist. Her stalker was still out there.

She lifted her chin, regaining her composure. "Whoever he is, I can lose him." She pressed on the accelerator and did a sharp right turn onto a side street. "It's funny, the shoe being on the other foot. I'll never again hound someone for a story. If they don't want to talk, they don't have to talk."

He craned his neck. "The guy is still with us."

She sped up and then zigzagged through a parking lot, pulling into a space. A few seconds later, the car zoomed by them.

"Good maneuver," he said. Without thinking, he reached over and lightly punched her shoulder.

Her expression changed at his touch. "I have a few." She yanked the gearshift into Reverse and pulled out of the parking space.

He shifted in his seat.

Despite the lightness of the interaction, the air between them was heavy with tension. They couldn't just be friends unless they were willing to talk about what had happened between then. He had no idea how to start that conversation.

"Maybe we shouldn't go back to my house," she said.

Was she thinking of the reporter—if it *was* a reporter—who might follow them there or had she decided that being alone with him was not safe?

"What do you suggest?"

She glanced in her rearview mirror. "There's a little café not too far outside of town. No one but locals know about it."

She took an exit and drove a few miles out of town. The warm glow emanating from the lights of the café came into view as she rounded a corner.

"My father used to take me here after we went fishing together," she said.

Maybe he was reading too much into her choice, but he liked that she had picked a place that she had a sentimental attachment to.

"You miss your father?"

She glanced at the ceiling and shook her head. "A great deal. My mom left when I was four. Daddy was my protector and my cheerleader. I'd send him a copy of the news stories I covered and he'd make his friends watch them."

"Sounds like a neat relationship."

They both opened their doors and went inside. The café had several people at the counter and two of the five tables were occupied. They slid into a booth and grabbed menus that were in the rack by the salt and pepper shakers.

"I guess the person I'm closest to would be my sister. She's the one who was responsible for getting me out of Syria before I was executed." Even saying the words caused his throat to tighten. But every time he talked about it, it got a little easier.

She set her menu down and studied him for a long while. "You were that close to death?"

Resistance settled around him, but he knew if he expected her to talk about the most painful thing in her life, he had to be willing to talk about his captivity. "Yes. God spared me for a reason. I owe Him my life so I gave it back to Him."

"Sometimes, though, you don't get justice and you're not spared." Her eyes glazed.

He felt a stab to his own heart. "I'm sorry for what happened to you. And I'm sorry I was out of line when I kissed you. I hope we can still be friends?"

She stared at him for a long moment, her expression giving nothing away. Maybe the pain was just too deep for her to even respond.

"What can I get you folks?"

He'd been so focused on Elizabeth, he hadn't even seen the waitress come up to their table.

"The burger and fries are good." Elizabeth cast her gaze down to the table.

"I'll have that, then. And a Coke."

"Make it two," she said.

The waitress walked away.

Elizabeth twirled the saltshaker and then set it down firmly. "Friends it is then."

Though he wanted so much more with her, if he only ever could be her friend, he'd be satisfied. "Let me cover the meal tonight. Since you are the one who came up with the escape plan."

She nodded.

He touched his pocket where his wallet should have been. "My wallet must have fallen out in the car. I'll be right back." He stepped outside into the dusky evening, opened the car door and felt around for his wallet. His hand touched leather. He stood up straight.

A hand went over his mouth, and the cold metal of a gun barrel stabbed into his side.

A voice like hardened steel pressed on him. "You're always in the way."

The waitress set two drinks down on the table. "What happened to your friend?"

"He just stepped out for a minute." Elizabeth's first thought was that he had skipped out on her. Which only showed how paper-thin her trust with men was. She knew Zach. She knew his character. And besides, where would he go? She was the one who'd driven them there.

Though she kept her tone casual, a deeper instinct told her that something might be wrong. "Could you excuse me for a minute?" She pulled a twenty out of her purse and put it on the table in case Zach had gotten cornered by someone, and they needed to leave in a rush.

She ran to the window of the café, but the angle was wrong to see her car. She opened the door and the cool evening breeze hit her. The *ka-thud ka-thud* of her heart surrounded her. She pushed past the rising panic and stepped outside, hurrying to where she'd parked the car.

The door on the passenger side was closed but not latched. She turned a quick half circle.

This didn't make any sense. The stalker was after her. Why would he have grabbed Zach? Maybe he hadn't, and this had something to do with the reporters who were hounding Zach. Had he slipped away to avoid them? Somehow, she didn't think that was what was going on. She sent him a quick text and watched her screen of a long moment. No reply.

She ran back inside. "Please call the sheriff. I think something has happened to my friend."

The lady behind the counter nodded. If the fear in Elizabeth's expression didn't tell her she was serious, the shakiness of her voice must have motivated the cashier to not question her.

Elizabeth darted back outside. She didn't have time to wait for law enforcement. She took off through the forest toward the logging camp—the only place nearby. It could be that Zach had been shoved into a car and taken somewhere, but she hadn't seen any cars pull up or leave.

She jumped over an old tire and ran toward the logging camp. She prayed that this was all some misunderstanding. But in her heart, she knew something had happened to her friend.

Zach struggled to come up with a way to subdue or escape from the man who had grabbed him. His kidnapper pushed him through the forest and out into an opening filled with broken, rusting equipment and dilapidated buildings.

Though his heart pounded wildly, he felt an inner calm that helped him think clearly. He'd had guns pointed at him before and had been in many situations where death seemed imminent. He could handle this. He just needed to wait for the moment of weakness when his captor's guard was down.

The kidnapper pushed Zach's shoulder. "Keep moving toward that building. Don't try anything or I will fill you with lead."

They walked past a pile of logs covered in moss. The buildings leaned to one side.

"In there, now," said the stalker.

What exactly did this guy have in mind? He'd implied that Zach was somehow impeding his access to Elizabeth. Would he really kill Zach just to get him out of the way?

Or was he bait?

He squeezed his eyes shut tight and opened them as fear struck a chord through him at the idea that he'd be used to get to Elizabeth and then killed. He prayed Elizabeth would wait for the authorities and not come looking for him on her own.

The man pointed. "Sit down there. Over in that corner."

In the dim light, Zach could just make out the man's face. He had a thick build where Zach was lean and tall. The guy could probably out-muscle him in a straight-on fight.

"I said sit down."

Zach complied even as his thoughts raced a hundred miles an hour. He sank down to the ground. "So what is your deal with Elizabeth?"

"Shut up." He paced and looked through the glassless window.

Zach's chest squeezed tight. Was this guy waiting for Elizabeth to show up, setting a trap for her?

Maybe if he could get the man stirred up, he'd lose his focus and give Zach an opportunity to get away before Elizabeth got here. In the meantime, he needed to find out as much as he could.

"So do you know Elizabeth?"

The man half turned in his direction. "We were meant to be together."

Clear signs of obsession. "She doesn't know you, though?"

"Shut up." The man dove toward him pressing the gun barrel against Zach's temple. "You don't know anything. You have no idea why I'm here."

Would pushing the man's buttons, placing the

truth in front of him, cause him to lose focus or would it make him more violent?

"I know that Elizabeth is a beautiful professional woman," Zach said.

"She doesn't like you." Her stalker spat out his words.

"How do you know that?" Zach intended his words to cut through the man's delusions. "I'm the one who spends time with her."

"She likes me. You need to stay away from her." He hit Zach on the back of the head with the barrel of the gun.

White-hot pain seared through his head. So getting the man riled was not a good choice. The man still loomed over him. He was at a disadvantage sitting on the ground.

Zach spoke through gritted teeth. "What are you waiting for? Shoot me already. Elizabeth is not stupid enough to stumble into your trap."

The man turned slightly, his shoulders slouching. Zach placed his weight on his hands and swung his leg out to hit the back of the bigger man's knees. As soon as he crumpled to the ground, Zach was on top of him. The two wrestled. Zach landed a blow to the man's cheek. Moonlight provided him with a clear view of the man's face just before he reared up and hit his forehead against Zach's. Bone crunched bone. Zach tumbled backward from the blow. Still reeling and unable to focus, he glimpsed a blurred figure running past the window. Elizabeth. The stalker saw her, too, and bolted after her.

Though he swayed from side to side, Zach pushed himself to his feet and chased after the man. He saw flashes of movement, indicating that Elizabeth was diving and hiding behind old equipment and then jumping up and running.

She had lured his attacker away from him with her tactics. Smart girl, but it made her a target. He had to get to her before the man did. As if aware of Zach's thoughts, the man turned around and shot at Zach. He dove behind a pile of logs as the bullet richocheted off metal.

His heart pounded in his chest. Adrenaline shot through him. He peered above the log. He could see the attacker shrouded in shadows, but he didn't spot Elizabeth anywhere.

A tap on his back caused him to jump and whirl around. Elizabeth placed her finger over her lips. He wanted to hug her. She'd been so smart in how she'd entered the camp and tricked her stalker.

He turned back around. The man was lumbering toward them. Zach did a hand gesture that indicated they should split off in separate directions. She nodded.

Maybe they could catch this guy, and it would

all finally be over for Elizabeth. Zach took off running, using the light color of the man's jacket to track his movement.

He couldn't see Elizabeth anywhere. He'd have to trust that she was able to stay one step ahead, as well. If they both jumped on him at the same time, they might be able to take him down and restrain him.

The stalker slipped behind a large piece of rusted metal. Zach sprinted toward it.

A gunshot shattered the silence. It hit the metal of the rusted truck behind him making a pinging noise. He dove to the ground and crawled soldier-style, seeking cover behind a steel cylinder. He couldn't see the man anymore.

He waited, listening for footfall. The evening breeze brushed over his skin. He scanned the entire camp. Silence. His heartbeat drummed in his ears. Where had they gone?

Their attacker had to be hiding, waiting for them to move. So he could shoot Zach and grab Elizabeth.

A minute passed. Zach studied the camp again, this time more slowly. He saw a flash of movement and then another as the man dashed toward Elizabeth. Zach sprinted across the camp. A gunshot whizzed past him. He kept running. In an effort to get away, Elizabeth crawled up on a piece of equipment that had a long conveyor belt connected to a slab of slanted metal.

The man raced to her, shaking the bottom of the belt until Elizabeth fell. Zach's heart seized up. He wasn't going to get to her in time. He watched as she was lifted off the ground. Elizabeth twisted her body and kicked in an effort to get away, but she couldn't dislodge the grip around her waist. The man lifted the gun with his free hand and aimed it at Zach.

Zach plunged to the ground. The stalker turned his back and was hauling Elizabeth deeper into the forest as Zach jumped to his feet and took off running. He willed his legs to move faster.

He prayed he would get to her in time.

TWELVE

Elizabeth twisted her body to break free of the man's iron grasp around her waist. Her arms as well were locked by his grip.

"Let me go."

He squeezed her tighter, lifting her feet off the ground. Where was he taking her?

In the distance, she heard sirens. The sheriff would go to the café first, and they were too far away to scream for help. He wouldn't get here in time.

"Please, stop hauling me. I'll do what you say."

"You lie, Elizabeth. You can't be trusted."

Her resistance seemed to feed his anger. She stopped struggling. Her body went limp. She caught a flash of motion to the side of her, Zach sneaking through the trees waiting for the right moment to jump the stalker.

She saw a black truck parked at a distance

along a country road. Once he got her in the truck, it would be over, little or no chance for escape.

She turned her head and sunk her teeth into the man's shoulder. His grip loosened enough so she could wiggle free. He grabbed for her, tearing her shirt. She sprinted four steps before his big hands clamped down on her shoulders. She swung around and kicked him in the shin.

Zach jumped on him from behind, taking the stalker to the ground. Elizabeth looked around for anything that could be used as a weapon. She picked up a stick and cracked it across the man's shoulders. The piece of wood broke, and the man continued to assault Zach, clamping his hands around Zach's throat.

"She belongs to me," he said through gritted teeth.

Panic shot through her. The man meant to strangle Zach.

Elizabeth wrapped her arm around the man's neck so his chin rested in her elbow and then she yanked backward. The man rose to his feet and shook Elizabeth off.

The sheriff emerged through the trees.

Their attacker took off running toward his truck, yanked open the door and jumped in, spitting gravel as he tore up the country road.

The sheriff fired a single shot that missed. The truck disappeared around a corner into the forest.

A moment later, the sheriff's SUV, probably driven by a deputy, appeared on the road. The sheriff ran up to the driver's-side window and pointed up the road where the truck had gone. The SUV sped away.

Zach stood beside Elizabeth. He turned to face her. "You all right?"

She was beaten up and out of breath. "I'll live." She felt as though her internal organs were shaking and vibrating.

"You handled yourself really smartly. You're not a bad fighter either."

Through the whole battle, she hadn't been afraid. Instead, her focus had been on defeating the man who'd brought terror back into her life. That was a change from the fear that controlled her before. "Yeah, but he got away." She didn't hold out a lot of hope that the deputy would catch up with him.

The sheriff strode over to them.

"I got a look at his face," Zach said. "I think I would be able to identify him if I saw him."

"I only caught glimpses," she said.

They stood shoulder to shoulder facing the sheriff.

"I'll let you know if my deputy catches up

with him." The sheriff tipped his hat. "I'm going to wait back at the café. We will need you two to come in and give statements."

The sheriff took the lead, walking in front of them. They walked side by side back to the café. The sheriff went in. She turned to face Zach.

"I suppose those burgers are stone cold by now." He stared down at her arm and touched her elbow lightly.

"I'm sure of it." She didn't jerk away from his touch. In fact, she wished there could be more between them. She knew Zach was a good man. But when he'd kissed her, all the old fears came back. Her head told her Zach was exactly who he appeared to be, but her heart just couldn't let him in.

She was struck all over again by the injustice and the unfairness of how her rapist was still controlling her life. Craig Miller should have gone to jail. Instead she was the one who was imprisoned.

"After we give our statements, why don't we grab something to go and you can drop me off at my place," he said, never taking his eyes off her.

The sadness washed over her like a wave and she pulled away. "Yes, let's do that."

They purchased some sandwiches and drove

back to town. As she eased by his apartment, she counted three news crews in the front and two in the back.

"They've got to go home sometime," said Zach.

"Why don't we go to the park and eat our food. Maybe they'll be gone by the time we're done." She circled the block and headed up the street.

"A couple more days and this will blow over."

She pulled her car into the lot. The park was virtually abandoned at this time of night. She found a flat, grassy spot beneath a tree. Zach handed her one of the to-go boxes. When she took the first bite of sandwich, she looked out across the park. A dark-colored truck eased by on the street.

Her back stiffened and she was alert, but the fear no longer overwhelmed her.

He scooted in close to her. "I see it, too. That truck is blue, not black."

"I will always be looking over my shoulder until that guy is in jail."

"I definitely think he's some sort of obsessed fan, judging from the things he said to me," Zach said. "He's delusional and unstable."

She felt a tightening through her rib cage.

Zach continued. "I don't want to scare you.

I just think you need to know what we're dealing with."

"I know." Resolve and fear wrestled within her. "His actions are confusing. Why didn't he kill me or take me when he had the chance when I was in the river? Why did he want to make sure I was scared at the country club?"

Zach shrugged. "It all messes with your mind—maybe that's his main goal. He seems a little obsessed with you, too."

Rain sprinkled from the sky and quickly became a downpour. They both jumped up from the grass, carrying their food and running toward a pavilion that provided shelter. Droplets pattered on the metal roof of the structure creating a restful rhythm.

They settled down on a picnic table that was under the pavilion, finishing their sandwiches and staring out at the rainfall. No words passed between them for a long time. She took the last bite of her food and closed the takeout container.

She scooted closer to Zach so their shoulders were touching. The longing for it to be more than just shoulders touching was always there. She didn't know how to navigate *that* fear.

But as she sat with her friend, a man she admired, she knew now she could get beyond her fear over the man who had abducted her. This stalker would not control her by being inside her head. She was stronger than all that, and she had a friend who was willing to stay by her side through all of it.

Elizabeth stared up at the monitor where the story she'd just edited was playing.

Wilson Degrasse, the weatherman, poked his head in the editing room. "See you tomorrow," he said. "Good broadcast tonight."

"We only make it happen by working together," she said.

Wilson gave her a fatherly smile. "You know I'm on the downside of my career." He touched his bald head. "Your talent deserves to be utilized in some place far greater than a little Podunk station in Montana."

She thought about it. She knew her career had been stalled out. First by what had happened in Seattle and then with taking care of her father. If things had happened differently… who could say? But that didn't mean she was unhappy where she was. "Guess I have fallen in love with Montana more than my career."

Wilson nodded. "Just remember, the scenery is part of your salary. Don't forget to set the alarms. You're the last one in the station."

"I've got a little more editing to do." She listened to the sound of Wilson's footfall on the carpet in the hall before turning her attention back to the footage of another story.

They were all slice-of-life and fluff pieces, but in a small town that was what most of the news was. The winning football team, the change in fishing or hunting regulations, the women's group that decided to help orphans halfway across the world.

Her phone rang. Zach. She clicked on. "Hey."

"How's the workload? I thought we could do some dinner."

"Can you bring some takeout to the station? I have just a little more to do before I can put this news day to bed," she said.

"See you in twenty."

In the two days since the attack at the logging camp, their lives had fallen into a comfortable routine of racing to news stories during the day. Both of them still able to get the friendly competitive barb in now and then. Sometimes they would eat dinner together and talk.

Her stalker was still out there. He hadn't been caught or identified. But Zach's description had at least allowed them to put together a drawing of the culprit. The black truck had not been found.

Going to each news story still caused her

angst, but she was able to hold it together. She was beginning to doubt the man would ever be caught.

She continued to view the footage of her news story. The buzzer on the security door sounded, and she unlocked it so Zach could come up to the second floor with their food. She sent out several emails concerning potential stories for the next week.

Her stomach growled. Zach sure was taking his sweet time. She went downstairs to where the administrative and ad sales desks were. No Zach.

She ran back up the stairs to get her phone and clicked in his number. "Zach, where are you?"

"Long line. I'm just getting back into my car. Gotta drive, can't talk." He hung up.

"Wait." He'd clicked off before hearing her protest. She stepped back from the black monitors as the hairs on the back of her neck stood on edge. If Zach hadn't arrived, then who had she let in?

She ran toward the door of the control room prepared to lock it and dial 911. The door slammed against the wall, and her stalker filled the doorway. He lunged at her. She skirted away from him but there wasn't much space to maneuver around the chairs and monitors.

Had he been waiting for the right moment when she was alone, watching her this whole time?

She backed into a corner. Her phone lay on the carpet. He crushed it with his foot and then reached his huge hands out for her. She swung at him. He grabbed her hand at the wrist and twisted her arm behind her back, pushing her arm up at an uncomfortable angle.

Zach was seven minutes away at the most. She could fight him off for that long.

Her attacker wrapped his arms around her. "Why won't you just come with me, Elizabeth? We were meant to be together."

Her heart raced but her mind was crystal clear. "Please, you're really hurting me."

"I don't want to hurt you. You *make* me hurt you because you won't do what I say."

"What do you want me to do?" Her gaze flicked up to the clock. How many minutes had passed? Two...or maybe three?

"You play games." He lifted her off her feet and hauled her through the door. He had her locked in his arms so tightly that she was almost immobile. "And now I'm in trouble."

She tried to drag her feet, digging in her heels. Her loafers fell off.

He pressed close to her ear, squeezing her

even tighter. "Stop it. You need to be good so we can be together just for a short time."

What did he mean by that? That he would kill her after that?

She was helpless to resist as he carried her through the station out the back door. He tossed her in the backseat of the black crew cab truck. Before she could recover, he leaned into the cab and placed duct tape on her mouth.

"Give me your hands."

She shook her head.

He slapped her once. Pain radiated from her cheek to the whole side of her face. Her eyes watered. While she was recovering from being hit, he grabbed her hands and wrapped the duct tape around them.

He landed another blow to her head. As consciousness faded, she wondered how long he would keep her alive before he decided to kill her.

THIRTEEN

Zach was surprised to find the security door unlocked, but thought that maybe Elizabeth had opened it knowing he was coming. Yet from the moment he stepped across the threshold, the atmosphere shifted. Something wasn't right.

He dashed up the stairs, calling out Elizabeth's name. He checked each room. Elizabeth's smashed cell phone was flung on the carpet of the control room.

His heart hammered a little faster as he sped downstairs. Her leather loafers were by the back door. When he flung open the door, he saw a black truck racing through the parking lot. Zach sprinted back to his own car and jumped in.

He headed up the street where he'd seen the truck going. Traffic was light at this hour, and it wasn't hard to spot the truck. As he drew close, the truck sped up and turned to head out of town, red taillights glowing like a monster's eyes.

If the truck hadn't figured out he had a tail, it would become obvious now. They were the only two cars on the road.

He thought to phone the police, but didn't want to risk slowing down to make a safe call. The truck zigzagged through the rural roads. Zach couldn't get close to him but at least he kept him in view.

The truck increased speed. Zach pressed down on the accelerator, going as fast as he dared on the gravel road. At too high a speed, the tiny rocks would act like marbles and flip his car.

The truck disappeared over a hill. When Zach rounded the crest, he saw no sign of the truck. He slowed, wondering if the kidnapper had turned off somewhere and killed the lights.

He drove a few hundred yards more and then turned around on a shoulder, scanning the dark landscape until moonlight picked up the glint of metal. Either this was a trap or the other man had gotten out of the truck and was dragging Elizabeth deeper into the trees. Either way Zach had to get to her quickly.

He killed his headlights and rolled toward where he'd seen the metal. He stopped when he figured he was close enough to be heard if a window was down in the truck.

He clicked open the door and slid down to the ground. He left the car door open. Using the brush as cover, he made his way toward the truck, circling around to the back. The stalker would be expecting to see him approach the cab.

He crouched and made his way to the back tire of the truck. Was the man in the truck or was he waiting in the woods, watching for the opportunity to jump Zach? Or was he already gone with Elizabeth—hauling her to some dark cave while Zach wasted time? He waited, not hearing anything.

His heart hammered out an intense rhythm. He scooted up closer to the cab, keeping one ear tuned to the sounds around him. He'd hear the man coming through the brush if that was how the game was going to be played.

When he peered into the cab, the front was empty. He flung open the door. Elizabeth was in the backseat, eyes wide with fear. His heart lurched just as the adrenaline kicked in. He knew the man was coming up from behind even before he heard him.

He swung around. The man held a log that he aimed at Zach's head. Zach ducked out of the line of trajectory but he wasn't able to move out of the shot entirely. The log hit his shoulder. The man swung again. This one knocked Zach back against the hard metal of the truck and drove the wind out of him. He sank to the ground. The man picked him up and set him to one side before he could recover.

Then the man got into the cab of the truck and ignited the engine. Zach bounced to his feet and took off in a run just as the truck chugged forward, managing to jump into the bed of the truck. The driver, spotting him, sped up to dangerously high speeds.

Zach could see Elizabeth in the back of the cab fully alert. The driver cut the wheel sharply back and forth on the road trying to throw him out. He turned off the road onto what was probably a dry river bottom. The truck bounced. Zach's teeth clamped on his tongue. He held on. A crowbar skittered past him in the bed of the truck.

Gunning the engine, they headed back up a steep incline toward the road. Zach lost his grip and slid toward the back of the truck. His spine impacted with the metal tailgate. The crowbar slid toward him. He grabbed it.

The truck leveled off, and he crawled back toward the cab. He leaned out to one side and hit the driver's-side window, causing it to spiderweb. He hit it three more times. One more blow and the driver would have a glass shower to contend with. Zach hung off the side of the truck at a dangerous angle and raised the crowbar.

The driver jerked the truck.

Zach's body impacted with a tree branch. He whirled through space and hit the ground hard. His vision blackened and then cleared.

His body screamed with pain. Only his heart cried louder as he watched the glaring red taillights of the truck that held Elizabeth fade into the distance.

Elizabeth watched as Zach flew off the back of the truck. She lifted her head to see better as her throat constricted. She could just make out the outline of his crumpled body on the ground beneath the tree. Her heart lurched. How badly was he hurt? Was he even alive?

He'd fought so hard to free her. She wasn't going to give up on herself.

She lifted her feet and kicked the back of the driver's head. He tried to dodge out of the way, which caused the truck to swerve. She kicked again.

He increased the speed of the truck and roared down the road.

"Quit that." He spoke through gritted teeth.

She sat up and slammed her duct-taped hands down on his shoulder.

"I said stop it, Elizabeth. Why can't you be nice to me?"

She wasn't going to stop. Rage seethed through her for what the man had done to Zach. She would use her anger to escape. This man was not going to hold her captive, and he wasn't going to kill her.

She hit him again.

He sped down the road at a dangerous velocity. She swayed, trying to maintain balance as he swerved.

He hit the accelerator hard. The road clipped by, blurring the scenery. He had to be going over a hundred miles an hour. She held her breath.

He stared straight ahead with a white-knuckle grip on the steering wheel. The anger inside the cab of the truck was almost palpable. Was he going to kill both of them?

She cringed. Maybe she'd made a mistake in fighting back.

The man was on edge and unstable.

Up ahead, the road curved but he showed no sign of slowing down. She braced for impact. She wasn't in a seat belt.

He let off on the accelerator at the last moment, swinging into the other lane of the curve. The truck fishtailed but remained on the road.

She was in the truck with a crazy man. What could she do? How would she get away?

He veered off the road into a grove of trees, hitting the brakes with force.

He pushed open the driver's-side door, stepped out and then yanked open the crew cab door. Even in the dim light, she saw that his face was red with rage. His teeth showed in a snarl.

She scooted as far away from him as she could on the seat.

He pointed his finger at her. "Don't hit me like that ever again, Elizabeth." He sounded hurt rather than angry.

He grabbed her foot and dragged her down the length of the seat. She tried to twist free of his grasp but she had no room to maneuver.

He grabbed her shoulders, reached up and ripped the duct tape off her mouth.

She thought to scream, but they had not passed anyone on the road who would hear, and it might set him off again.

He pulled a plastic-wrapped packet out of his shirt pocket that he unfolded to reveal three pills. "Take these."

She shook her head.

He folded the packet back up and put it in

his pocket. His sudden calmness was eerie; the mood changes hinted at how unstable he was.

Her muscles tensed as she watched his every move.

He sprang on her, clamping his hands on her throat and pressing. Her world went darker than the night that surrounded her.

Pain seared through every muscle as Zach pushed his bruised body up. He leaned against the tree for support and pulled out his phone.

He dialed his detective friend's private number. Glenn picked up on the first ring.

He didn't even give Glenn a chance to talk. "Listen, Elizabeth Kramer has been kidnapped by that nut case. I'm out on Garrison Road not too far from the Clear Creek fishing access. They were headed due east."

"I'll get a team on it."

He'd had the presence of mind to pay attention to the license number on the truck. "You need to run a plate for me." He dictated the numbers. "We've got to figure out who this guy is and then we can figure out where he's taken Elizabeth."

"I'll get the whole force on it."

"We can't move fast enough." His voice faltered at the thought of losing Elizabeth. "When you get out this way, pick me up."

He clicked off the phone, praying that they weren't already too late.

Elizabeth awoke feeling groggy. Her head hurt. She was on some kind of cot in a room with dark curtains. She stumbled and swayed when she stood up. Her captor must have forced the pills down her throat after he'd caused her to pass out.

When she tried the door, it was locked. She pulled back the curtains only to discover that the windows were boarded up from the outside. The room smelled musty. She was still barefoot.

She heard a faint voice on the other side of the door. She pressed closer. She could make out pacing—and the way the floor shook. They were in a trailer or something with a flimsy floor.

She only heard one voice. Her captor must be talking on the phone.

She sank down to the floor and tuned her ear to the one-sided conversation. Judging from the tone, he was obviously upset.

She heard a flurry of phrases. "But you said I could be with her. I don't think it worked like you wanted... That's not my fault."

It sounded like Stalker had a partner.

The room grew silent and then she heard

footsteps coming back toward the door. She jumped in the bed and pretended to be asleep.

The door slid open. She kept her eyes shut, even though she could smell him as he stood close, a dirt-and-grease stench. His gaze was like weight on her skin. Then his hand brushed over her hair.

Inwardly, she cringed but managed not to openly react to his touch. He placed a pair of shoes on her feet. Several minutes passed before she heard his retreating footsteps. The door clicked as the lock slid into place.

She sat up and looked around. What was here that she could use to escape? The man had to sleep and go out for supplies sometime. The room was pretty bare-bones. Just a bed and nightstand. When she opened the drawer, she found a pen and paper, nothing else.

She pulled back the black curtain and slid the window open. She hurried across the room and listened at the door. It sounded like the television was on. She went back to the window and pushed against the plywood. It had a little give to it, which she hoped meant it wasn't nailed on very firmly.

Elizabeth pushed against the plywood putting all her weight into it. The wood bowed a little but didn't give way.

The television went off and the distinct ringing of a phone caused her to back away from the window.

She could hear the man stomping across the floor. He was shouting so she was able to catch most of the conversation.

"What do you mean? That wasn't part of the deal. You said I could have her for a while."

There was a long pause. And then he said something in a much lower tone. The room fell silent. After a long moment, he spoke. "I'm not a killer. That wasn't part of the deal."

Elizabeth shivered.

The door burst open. The man's face was red with rage. He grabbed her arm. "You're coming with me."

She pulled away and dashed for the open door, running through a small living room and twisting the knob to the outside door. He came up behind her just as the door swung open. She spied a baseball bat by the door, picked it up and swung it at his head. The man reeled backward and collapsed to the floor, still conscious but clearly in pain.

She jumped down the stairs. She was surrounded by forest. No chance of calling for help. She took off running. A quick check in the cab of the truck revealed that the keys were not in the ignition. Her gaze darted toward the open door of the trailer. The man still hadn't recovered. She swung open the truck door, flipped down the visor and felt for the keys. No luck.

Her attacker was on his feet now, looming in the doorway. She took off running toward the forest. He wouldn't be able to follow her in the truck. He was a big man, hopefully not very fast. She prayed she could outrun him.

FOURTEEN

Zach gripped the armrest of the police SUV. The tension in his body and his racing thoughts made it hard to pray. The police car seemed to be moving at a snail's pace toward the remote area in the forest where the stalker apparently lived. At least they'd let him ride along. The license plate on the truck had given them a name and address. Kenny Davis, a man with a history of mental illness, part-time construction worker and hunting guide.

They rounded a curve, and the trailer came into view. The door to the trailer was open as was the door to the truck. The two officers in the front seat piled out with their weapons drawn as did the men in the police car behind them. Zach jumped out of the SUV, crouched close to it and surveyed the area.

Two of the officers stormed into the trailer. The third officer peered into the truck while the fourth searched around the building.

The two officers emerged from the trailer, shoulders slumped, weapons no longer drawn. He could guess at what had transpired based on the open doors. Elizabeth had escaped the trailer and then tried—and failed—to leave in the truck.

What he didn't know was if she'd been caught by Kenny or not. The truck was still here. So she must've run where a truck couldn't go.

Zach headed toward the forest. The officers knew he wasn't going to sit idly by while Elizabeth might be fighting for her life. They could follow him or not. He didn't care. All he wanted was to find Elizabeth alive.

He came to the edge of the woods and looked over his shoulder just in time to see Neil Thompson's news van pulling up. *Oh, great.*

One of the other officers caught up with him. "We're minutes behind them. One of the burners in the trailer was still warm. I'm going to see if I can get some chopper support. The officers here will enter the forest twenty yards apart to do a search."

Zach turned a half circle taking in the terrain. "If they'd headed out in the open country, we'd see them. Wherever they are, the choppers won't be able to spot them. I'm going to help look for her."

The officer patted Zach on the back, indicating that he was fine with that.

Zach knew the risk he was taking. Kenny was unstable, and he was probably armed. Zach didn't care. His yearning to make sure Elizabeth was alive and safe overtook any fear he had. Knowing that she might be hurt created a hollow space inside him. He loved her even if she couldn't love him back.

He headed into the forest, praying they weren't too late.

Elizabeth ran as fast as she dared across the rough terrain. The wooded area had quickly given way to rocky outcroppings. She glanced over her shoulder. Her stalker was in clear view and closing in on her.

She jumped around a scattering of rocks and searched the landscape for the clearest path. Her foot caught on a rock. She stumbled but righted herself before she did a face-plant.

Her attacker was twenty yards behind her. Close enough that if he had had a gun he could have shot her.

Up ahead, she could see more forest and easier footing. She took careful quick steps over a slab of rock. She ran faster when her feet hit solid ground. Once in the forest, she came to a marked trailhead and bolted up it, though she knew she'd have to veer off the trail at the first opportunity to evade her pursuer.

She pushed herself up the terraced trail where bare tree roots formed steps.

"Elizabeth, don't run away from me." The agony-filled voice came from below her. She pushed hard up the steep landscape, seeking for an opening in the trees that would allow her to disappear from her stalker's line of sight.

The trail rounded a curve so the view from below was limited. She darted back into the trees, losing all sense of direction. Finding a road or a river to follow out would come later. Right now she needed to put distance between herself and her pursuer.

The climb was steep. She steadied herself by holding on to the narrow lodgepole pines that grew in the hillside. Her legs burned from the effort and she fought for breath.

Just get away from him.

After she worked her way up the hill, she stopped to catch her breath. The breaking of branches drew her attention. Before she could absorb what it indicated, hands with an iron grip clamped on to her arm.

Her stalker's face was very close to hers. "Did you think I don't know these woods?" He yanked her even closer. "Every shortcut. Every side trail. I live here."

Her heart thudded in her chest. She fought against rising terror. He was ten times stronger than her. She had to win this battle by manipulating his mind, playing on his obsession with her. "Please, I'm so sorry I ran away."

"Sure you are. You're bad, Elizabeth."

"I'll do what you say. I promise."

"It's too late for that." He jerked her up the mountain.

She scanned the area around her. If she could just get away for a second, she could pick up a rock or a stick.

"You hurt me, Elizabeth. You hurt me bad." His voice filled with rage. "I don't want to do this to you." In an instant, his voice indicated pain. "But I have to keep my word."

He dragged her up the hill. Something seemed to have shifted for him. She remembered the phone conversation where it had sounded as if he was taking orders from someone. "Whatever you have planned, you don't have to go through with it."

"I wanted us to be together. Why couldn't you just be good, Elizabeth? At least we can die together."

His words chilled her to the bone, but her mind remained clear. She planted her feet and tried to pull away. He tightened his grip on her arm. Her skin burned from the pressure.

"What's going on? Is someone making you do this?"

His expression grew dark, and he slapped her face. She doubled over from the pain. He pulled her up the hill as her feet dragged along the forest floor.

"Did somebody put you up to this? Maybe I can help you."

His tone softened a little. "I know the game you're playing. I thought you were a good girl, Elizabeth."

She tried to twist away. He dumped her on the ground. She turned first to the hill they'd just climbed and then to the sudden drop off and the jagged rocks below. Her heart beat even faster. She saw in his eyes what he intended.

"I have no choice. You're bad. You didn't do what you were supposed to do."

She flipped over and crawled away, struggling to get to her feet. He grabbed her collar and yanked her back toward the edge of the sheer drop-off.

He swung her around. She stared down the steep incline. Every muscle in her body had turned to stone.

She forced the words up her throat. "Please, don't." Even as she spoke, she could imagine her body falling through the air and bouncing off the rocks.

His grip lightened a little.

"I'll be good. I promise."

"It's too late." He pressed on her shoulder. "We'll die together."

She took a step back as rocks and dirt cascaded down the cliff.

He lifted her up by the waist as though he were going to toss her like a ball. She screamed and kicked. He drew nearer to the cliff.

Please, God, help me.

She screamed again. The ground below her disappeared. She saw rocks and her life ending. Her last thought was of Zach and that he would never know how much she cared about him.

Zach heard Elizabeth's screams from halfway down the mountain. He pushed through the thick undergrowth, pumping his arms and legs. When he came out into the open, he saw Kenny dangling Elizabeth over the edge of a mountain.

He darted across the open area and body-slammed Kenny. All three of them rolled down the incline of the hill away from the cliff. Kenny grabbed Zach by the collar with one hand and punched him with the other. He landed a second blow to his stomach, which made Zach double over.

With the wind knocked out of him, Zach

took a moment to recover. When he looked up, Kenny was dragging Elizabeth back over to the cliff face.

"I'm a witness, Kenny. Don't do this—you don't want to go to jail."

"There'll be no witnesses." The look in Kenny's eyes was crazed. Was it even possible to reason with this man?

Kenny's arms wrapped completely around Elizabeth, locking her arms in place. Elizabeth looked at Zach, eyes pleading.

Zach eased his way closer. "You don't want to do this, Kenny."

"I wanted Elizabeth and me to be together. This is the only way."

Kenny swung in a half circle, so Elizabeth dangled over the cliff edge. Zach lunged at Kenny kicking the back of his knees. Kenny crumpled to the ground, letting go of Elizabeth. Zach caught Elizabeth's hand. Kenny was on top of them. Zach landed a blow hard across Kenny's jaw and then administered a jab to Kenny's throat that made him gasp for air. Kenny fell on his side clutching his neck.

Knowing he had only seconds before Kenny recovered, he grabbed Elizabeth's hand and took off running. They made it ten yards before Kenny hurled a rock at Elizabeth's back and she went down.

Kenny closed the distance between them. Despite the difference in their sizes, Zach went after him, managing to knock him to the ground, stunned, by slamming a log against the back of Kenny's head.

Zach pulled Elizabeth up. They ran down the mountain. He saw movement through the trees. The police were down below, but not within shouting distance. The terrain evened out some though none of it looked familiar. It was too much of a risk to get back on the trail. Kenny would find them too easily.

They ran through the woods in what he thought was the general direction of the trailer, where he knew he'd find the police. He waited for something to look familiar.

Elizabeth gripped his arm. "Behind us."

Kenny was moving through the forest surprisingly fast for a man his size. Then again, his rage and delusion probably fueled his strength.

The trees opened up to rockier terrain. Zach ran only with the intent of getting away from Kenny. Elizabeth kept pace with him. The rock turned to shale and a treacherous loose rock caused them to lose their foothold, sliding hundreds of feet. He could not tell up from down. Rocks hit and bruised his body as he rolled through space until the ground evened out and he came to a stop. The dust cleared. He saw

Elizabeth's prone body twenty feet away. He crawled toward her, praying that she was alive.

Elizabeth opened her eyes. Zach's arms cradled her as the dust settled around her. She let out a breath waiting for her heart to slow down.

His hands warmed her cheeks. "You all right?"

"My head hurts and it feels like I was in a dryer with bricks."

He laughed. "Close enough." His knuckles brushed over her cheek. A more-than-friendly gesture, but she didn't recoil from his touch. "Are you okay to walk?"

She nodded.

"I think we shook Kenny but we've gotten way off course." He turned slightly away from her. "We can't climb back up that way."

"How far are we from the trailer?"

He craned his neck, looking around. "I'm not sure. The police are at the trailer and I saw them in the trees. It seems like they would have brought in search and rescue by now."

How far, she wondered, had they veered off from the predictable path. Would search and rescue even be looking for them in this part of the forest?

Zach tilted his head. "I haven't seen any air support either."

Every muscle screamed in agony as she pushed herself into a sitting position. "Let's just keep moving. They'll find us or we'll find them."

Or Kenny would find us.

Kenny had seen where they'd gone and probably knew a way around the shale.

She rose to her feet. He reached out a hand for her and led her through the trees and across an open area. Nothing looked familiar in descending darkness. If they could make it until daylight without running into Kenny, they had a fighting chance of getting out of the forest alive. If only she could believe they actually would...

Zach backed up to a tree and pulled her to him. He made a shushing noise. Now she heard it. The sound of footsteps. Someone moving through the forest. She pressed close to Zach, her hand on his chest. His heartbeat pushed back against her palm.

The footsteps grew louder. If it had been a policeman, he would have a flashlight. She held her breath when a dark, hulking figure passed them—then stopped walking and turned in their direction.

She squeezed her eyes shut and stood as still as a statue.

Please, God, don't let him see us.

A long moment passed before the footsteps continued then faded. Even after the human noises faded, she and Zach remained, still facing each other, not daring to move. His breath was soft on her face. She felt herself relax. She tilted her head.

"It would be all right if you kissed me," she whispered.

He kissed her forehead so gently, it felt like butterfly wings brushing her skin. Then his lips touched the tip of her nose. Her heart fluttered with a mixture of fear and excitement. His mouth covered hers as light as a feather, and she felt herself melt into his touch. He kissed her again tenderly.

Despite the danger they were in, the world felt completely safe as long as she was with Zach. Her hand rested against his chest as she tuned in to the beating of his heart. Everything else seemed to fall away and nothing else mattered.

He kissed her again on the forehead and drew her close. "I'll get you out of here alive, Elizabeth. Whatever it takes."

"I know you will."

He held her for a long moment. She relished the warmth of his embrace and wished that she could stay in this moment forever.

He whispered in her ear. "We know which

direction he went. So we'll move in the opposite direction."

That might not get them to the trailer, but avoiding Kenny was more important. They headed back through the forest and the encroaching darkness. Both of them stepping carefully, trying to make as little noise as possible.

His hand slipped into hers. The warmth of his touch radiated through her skin straight to the marrow of her bones. Him holding her hand felt like the most natural thing in the world.

They made their way through the dense trees and undergrowth. Zach pulled her back as she heard the sound of rocks and dirt falling by her feet.

She stared down into a deep hole. "What is this?"

Zach looked over the edge. "Maybe someone had a mining claim."

The *whop whop whop whop* of a helicopter broke the silence of the forest.

She tilted her head unable to see anything but tree branches.

"We need to get out in the open so they can see us." He grabbed her hand and ran.

Tree branches seemed to be everywhere, slowing their progress. The helicopter sounded like it was getting louder. She spied an opening to her right and ran toward it. As the forest thinned, she increased her speed.

The trees opened up into a grassy meadow.

They both jumped up and down and waved their arms.

The helicopter banked and turned in the opposite direction.

She shouted and waved her arms anyway even as hope ebbed.

The mechanical clang of the helicopter became less distinct and then faded altogether.

Elizabeth shrank back toward Zach, and the quiet surrounded them once again.

"Let's go toward where it went," Zach said.

She appreciated that he was trying to remain positive. She turned to face him just in time to see the shadow behind him that raised a thick log and brought it down on Zach's head.

FIFTEEN

Zach heard Kenny's approaching footsteps and whirled around. He blocked the blow with the log by putting his arm up. Pain burned down his arm. The two men covered some ground as they exchanged blows, but Kenny finally drove Zach down, then grabbed Elizabeth by the collar and dragged her away.

"Let go of her." Zach fought to recover and get to his feet. He wasn't going to let Elizabeth die here today.

She clawed at Kenny's hands as the fear in her eyes intensified. Zach reached out for her as he fought past the images of losing her.

Kenny wrapped his arm around Elizabeth's neck. "Come any closer and I'll just break her neck right now. It doesn't matter—nothing matters anymore."

The terror Zach saw on her face made him crumple inside.

Elizabeth spoke in a calm voice. "Do what he says. It'll be a *whole* lot better for both of us."

Zach wasn't sure what Elizabeth had in mind, but he held his hands up and took a step back. "I'm backing off." She had emphasized the word *whole*...meaning *hole*! He had to find a way to lead Kenny back to the hole.

Kenny hoisted Elizabeth over his shoulders and disappeared into the trees. Though he couldn't be sure, Zach thought he was headed in the direction of the cliff face where he had wanted to kill himself and Elizabeth earlier. He hadn't saved Elizabeth's life by backing off, only bought her time.

Zach saw flashes of color as he followed Kenny through the trees. Zach moved with stealth, careful not to give himself away. Several times, Kenny stopped, dumped Elizabeth on the ground and stood listening. Zach pressed himself against the tree not even daring to breathe. Kenny must know that Zach would follow them.

Elizabeth tried to crawl away. Kenny grabbed her foot and dragged her back to him. She kicked Kenny in the face and struggled to her feet. Zach burst through the trees and grabbed her hand.

He had only seconds to orient himself to where the hole was. He let go of her hand, so they both could go faster. Kenny was right on top of them.

Zach recognized the boulder they'd passed right before the hole. They entered the grove of trees. He kept running though he couldn't see Elizabeth. She had to be close. He could hear Kenny behind him. Then he saw a flash of color in his peripheral vision. Elizabeth. He heard her scream. And then Kenny screamed. Zach darted to where the hole was. Both of them had fallen in.

Kenny had become rabid. Clawing at the soil and roots jutting out the side of the hole and then lunging at Elizabeth as she tried to climb out. He pulled her down to the bottom of the hole and jumped on top of her, his arms around her neck.

Frantic, Zach searched from something to throw at Kenny to get him off Elizabeth. Elizabeth sank her teeth into Kenny's hand. Kenny yowled in pain as Zach picked up a rock and threw it at Kenny's shoulder.

Elizabeth used the distraction to race toward the side of the hole where she might be able to climb out. She'd made it halfway before Kenny had recovered and grabbed her feet.

Zach reached down. Their hands were only inches apart. Kenny pulled on her foot while she anchored herself to a root with one hand

and reached for Zach with the other. He dare not back off to find a tree branch to hold out to her. At the risk of falling in, he leaned over even more and grasped her hand. He could feel the blood rush to his head as he tried to pull himself back up and hold on to her. She reached up and grabbed another root.

Kenny had to jump to try to grip her foot.

Rocks and dirt cascaded down the hole as Zach strained to yank Elizabeth up. Elizabeth grasped for his other hand. He leaned back and pulled her up. Down below, Kenny groaned and clawed the sides of the hole and then placed his hand on his ears and rocked back and forth.

Zach held her tightly in his arms. "I thought I was going to lose you."

She clung to him, gripping his shoulder with her hand.

He heard noises behind him. A police officer emerged from the trees and ran up to them.

Still holding Elizabeth close, Zach tilted his head. "He's down there."

"We'll get a rescue crew in here." The officer walked a few paces away from them and spoke commands into his radio.

Within minutes, the helicopter had landed. Search and rescue showed up shortly after that. Kenny was pulled out of the hole and forcibly sedated.

Elizabeth stayed close to Zach while Kenny's limp body was put in a litter a lifted up by the rescue team. They carried a conscious but sedated Kenny to the chopper and loaded him in.

The officer approached Zach and Elizabeth. "There's room in the chopper. It'll get you to town faster than anything else. I'm sure you folks have been through enough and would like to be out of these trees."

While the blades sliced the air and overwhelmed all other sound, Zach and Elizabeth jumped into the two available seats. Kenny lay on the stretcher behind them. The chopper lifted into the air. The forest, deep hole and the rescue crew grew smaller and smaller.

Zach's hand slipped into Elizabeth's. She squeezed his fingers.

The nightmare was over. She was safe.

He remembered the kiss they'd shared. Maybe they might have a life together as more than friends.

The helicopter gained altitude. Within minutes, the outskirts of Badger came into view.

An arm came up from behind and wrapped around Elizabeth's neck as a syringe rolled around on the floor of the chopper. Kenny must have shot himself full of adrenaline from the first aid kit.

"She's mine," a crazed Kenny shouted. "We'll be together forever."

He pulled Elizabeth toward the door of the chopper.

Alert to the situation, the pilot banked the other way. Kenny and Elizabeth crashed against the wall of the helicopter. Zach pulled Elizabeth forward, but Kenny fell backward toward the open door of the helicopter. He disappeared as he slid out. Zach hurried across the short length of the chopper. Kenny clung to one of the runners of the helicopter. The wind intensified to hurricane force as Zach reached out a hand to help Kenny.

Kenny stared down at the ground below. Was he thinking of suicide? He seemed to want that only if he could take Elizabeth with him. It didn't matter what Kenny had done. His life meant something to God. Zach leaned out of the chopper and grabbed Kenny's hands.

Elizabeth grabbed hold of Zach's feet, so he wouldn't slip out. The pilot tilted the chopper to enable them to pull Kenny in. Once inside, Kenny collapsed. The adrenaline must be wearing off. He'd lost his will to fight.

"Let's get him tied up. That should have happened in the first place."

They worked together to turn Kenny over and restrain him. They climbed back into their seats. Elizabeth's hand intertwined with his.

The helipad on the hospital roof came into view. The pilot brought the helicopter down to the landing pad. Before the blades had stopped spinning, a crew of nurses and doctors appeared.

Kenny was loaded onto a gurney.

A nurse reached out her hand to Elizabeth. "Let's get you both inside and checked out."

Zach followed them into the ER. The nurse pulled curtains to create private exam space. "Each of you can take a room. A doctor will be with you shortly."

Elizabeth grabbed Zach's arm, leaned in and kissed him on the cheek. The look of pure affection in her eyes warmed him to the marrow of his bones. They'd come so far. She trusted him. She cared about him. He'd go through the whole ordeal again, if it was what it took for her to open her heart to him.

She let go of him and disappeared behind the curtain wall. Zach hoisted himself up on the exam table and stared at the ceiling. Praising God that the ordeal was finally and truly over.

Though she knew Kenny was incapacitated, anxiety coiled inside her like a cobra waiting to strike. The only thing that had eased her worry was being close to Zach. When she was with him, she felt like whatever they faced they could conquer as long as they were together. And she knew there *was* still another danger to face.

Kenny had been taking orders from someone. And she still needed to find out who.

The curtain slid open. A male nurse stepped in. "I heard you had quite the ordeal, Miss Kramer. Do you mind if I examine you?"

She'd jumped when he appeared. Her heart hammered in her chest. The man was in his early forties and had a genuine smile. Still, old fears returned.

"Actually, I think I would prefer to have a female nurse do the exam," she said.

He studied her for a moment before nodding. "I totally understand. It'll be just a few minutes."

She waited, listening to medical staff joking and barking orders, the beeping of machines and carts being rolled across the industrial-strength floor. There had been no time to tell Zach of her suspicions. She hoped they would have a chance soon. Even talking to him would alleviate much of her fear.

An older woman with bright blue eyes poked her head past the curtain. "Elizabeth?"

She nodded.

The nurse stepped into the room and studied Elizabeth for a moment. "At the very least you have lots of cuts and bruises that we need to deal with."

She was grateful that the nurse seemed like a kind grandmother. The exam went quickly, and Elizabeth got dressed and found the admit desk to fill out her paperwork. While the clerk waited for documents to print, she looked around for Zach. Certainly, he wouldn't have left without her.

"Here you go." The clerk shoved several pages toward her.

She read them in a cursory way before signing them.

Zach's voice filled the air around her. "Are you about ready to go?"

She nodded, feeling dizzy when he was so close. She reached out and brushed her hand over his forearm. "Two minutes."

She turned back to finish with the paperwork. He stood close to her. She'd let him into her life further than any man other than her father in the past ten years. Despite how wonderful she felt around him, how safe, she knew there were still walls. Her reaction to the male nurse revealed that. Fear lingered in the back of her mind, and she wondered if marriage would ever be a possibility for her. As wonderful as these feelings were, maybe it wasn't right to lead Zach on.

Zach pointed toward the main entrance of the ER. "There are a couple of news crews outside."

She let out a huff of air. "I never intended to have this kind of attention focused on me."

"We can get out over by the laundry facilities. One of my EMT buddies loaned me his car so I can take you home."

They hurried through the hospital and out into a back parking lot. Zach pulled the keys from his pocket, and she got into the passenger side. "I checked on Kenny's status. He's still unconscious."

They were five minutes from her house when she finally found the courage to speak up. "I have reason to believe that Kenny was not working alone. I think someone sent him after me."

"Why would he have to be sent? The police told me they found recordings of your newscasts in his trailer. There was footage of him in a crowd at a news story you covered. He was an obsessed fan—it's as simple as that."

"Here's one complication—I heard him talking to someone on the phone when I was in that trailer. They were discussing me, and the person on the other end seemed to be giving Kenny orders. It makes sense that Kenny couldn't have been the one orchestrating all of this. You saw his mental state. He must have had help."

Zach shrugged. "We'll let the police know." He parked the car by her house and turned to face her. He reached out to touch her cheek. "We've got to get on with our lives."

His expression softened. The nuance of affection his words carried cut her to the core. He thought they had a future together. She wanted that more than anything. And she certainly didn't want to hurt this kind, brave man. Deep down, though, she knew her damage would make it hard to move forward in the relationship.

"You don't believe me about Kenny having help?"

He gripped the steering wheel. His jaw hardened. "I want to believe this is over for you." Pain filled his voice. "You've been through enough."

"Maybe when Kenny regains consciousness, he'll talk." She could feel the wedge being driven between them. This wasn't just about Kenny. She pushed open the car door.

He got out and met her on the sidewalk. His

hand touched her elbow. "Maybe we can have dinner later."

She turned to look at him. He must have seen something in her face because his expression changed.

"Or maybe not," he said.

"You're...beyond special to me. But I just can't be in a relationship. I don't think I can ever be married and that would be the reason for us to date."

He lifted his hand, palm facing her. She leaned toward him, signaling that it was okay for him to touch her. His hand rested softly on her cheek. "I understand. You'll always be my friend." Pain and disappointment saturated his words.

She took a step back, feeling as though she might fall apart. She stood on the sidewalk watching him get into his borrowed car and drive away. She touched her cheek where his hand had been. She watched as he turned a corner and disappeared. Her heart was heavy as she made her way up the sidewalk and back into her house. Back to her old life of putting all her energy into her job.

Once inside, she shut the door and collapsed on the floor, weeping over all that had been stolen from her.

She sat up, leaned her back against the couch,

wiped her eyes and stared out the window. She had a more immediate threat to think about. Kenny had had help. That much she knew. This was not over yet.

SIXTEEN

Elizabeth stared at the text from Dale.

Possible fire at the old sugar beet factory. Meet me there in twenty.

She grabbed her bag that contained everything she needed to cover a story and headed out the door.

She slipped behind the wheel and took in a breath. The first exciting-sounding story since she'd told Zach three days ago there could never be an "us" for them. She hadn't seen him since. Maybe he'd been staying away from the fluffy stories on purpose.

Even the thought that she'd hurt him made it feel like someone had punched her in the stomach. She started the car. Then pulled her phone out to text Zach.

Before they had been competitors. Now they were friends. In the past, she would have relished getting the scoop on him. Now she wanted to help him.

She clicked on the letters on the tiny screen.

Possible fire at the sugar beet factory. Headed there now. Telling you this as a friend.

She tossed her phone back in the bag and pulled away from the curb. She missed him as a friend and someone who understood the crazy business they were in. If he showed up, maybe it would indicate he was ready to resume their friendship.

She drove out of town past flat, rolling fields of grain. The sugar beet factory hadn't been operable for years though there was probably plenty there that could catch on fire.

She felt a moment of fear at the memory of the last fire she'd covered, but pushed past it with the reminder that there had been no attacks against her since Kenny Davis had been caught.

Kenny had regained consciousness, but between the mental illness and the medication not much of what he said made sense. They had learned that the truck he'd driven was a recent purchase and way out of his price range. Maybe that was an indication that he was working for someone. But whoever it was didn't seem to want to confront her in person, so she should be safe. Mostly.

The sugar beet factory came into view. She drove through the security gate, broken years before by teenagers who came out here to party. She brought her car to a stop as the hairs on the back of her head stood on end. No fire truck. No police. No other news teams. No Dale. She never beat the first responders to a story. What was going on here?

She opened her door and studied the abandoned buildings. Then she saw it. Flames shooting out of the second story of one of the buildings. She heard shouting inside.

"Help me! Help me!"

Elizabeth bolted up the stairs. The flames spread across the floor and shot out the window but had not consumed the entire building. "Is somebody in here?"

She heard the voice again coming from the room behind the one that was on fire.

"Help me, please. I can't move!"

She grabbed a welder's coat that was hanging on the wall and beat back the flames enough so she could get through. She ran toward the closed door. When she jiggled the handle, it didn't budge.

"I'm coming in there." She turned sideways and slammed her hip against the aging door. It burst open. The room contained debris, empty beer and pop cans. There wasn't a person in sight.

Her heart hammered in her chest as she walked across the worn wooden floorboards and picked up the tape recorder sitting on the floor.

A voice played through the speakers. "Help me! Help me! Help me, please. I can't move!"

All the air left her lungs. She turned to escape the tiny room, but the path was full of growing flames. She slammed the door shut and ran toward a broken window, jumping out to land on the tires and other pieces of equipment that were stacked below.

She sprinted back toward where she'd left her car,

What sort of sick game was going on here? Kenny was locked away. Was this someone playing a joke or was this the person who'd been assisting Kenny?

Elizabeth heard footsteps behind her. When she looked over her shoulder, a man wearing a ski mask was twenty paces behind her. She ran faster.

He gained on her. His hand clamped her shoulder and yanked her back. The man was the same build as Neil Thompson.

She swung around and kicked him hard

in the shin. He bent over, but recovered and lunged at her, only tightening his grip when she struggled. He dragged her back to her car. When the man tried to shove her in the backseat, she started hitting him over and over and then reached up to pull off his mask. The move seemed to infuriate him. His fist slammed into the side of her head and then punched her hard in the gut several times.

With the wind knocked out of her, she was helpless to respond. He lifted her up and shoved her in the backseat as she wheezed and gasped for air. He got into the driver's seat and sped out of the factory grounds. The back tires spat gravel as he drove at a dangerous speed.

After a few minutes, she was able to take in a breath. She sat up. "Neil, you can't really want to do this. It's only a job."

The man didn't respond.

"I know who you are." Again she reached for his mask.

He slammed on the brakes in the middle of the country road. While he was getting out, she pushed open the door opposite him. As soon as her feet hit the dirt of the road, she dashed off toward the open field.

He ran after her.

She sprinted, increasing her stride. Her legs burned from the effort. The man lunged at her and took her down to the ground. The two wrestled. She twisted free and landed a hard blow to his face. She tried to crawl away on all fours but he grabbed her ankle and dragged her back.

She sat up and reached for his mask again, clawed at it as he angled to get away. All the strength and every ounce of fight left her body when she saw who her attacker was.

Craig Miller, the man who had ruined her life ten years ago.

She struggled to take in a breath.

His voice dripped with sarcasm. "Elizabeth, now you've gone and ruined everything."

She was like a rag doll as he dragged her back to the car. She thought she might faint. Against this man, she had no fight in her.

Zach stared at Elizabeth's text for only a moment before he knew something was wrong. He would have heard from the first responders if there was a fire anywhere. This had to be a trap. He tried to call her, but there was no answer. The text had come in ten minutes earlier, while he'd been in the shower—was he already too late?

He jumped in his car and drove out to the sugar beet factory pushing it to high speeds on the two-lane. He'd just heard the news from his cop friend that Kenny Davis had been released from custody on some technicality. The turn of events was so recent that Elizabeth probably hadn't been contacted yet.

Though Zach had meant it when he said he would always be her friend, he'd been avoiding Elizabeth, not going to the stories where he expected to run into her or waiting until he knew she was gone. They would be friends again, but right now seeing her was just too painful.

If she was in trouble though, he needed to get to her. He would always love her even if she couldn't love him back. As he approached the sugar beet factory, he saw Elizabeth's little red compact car pulling out. He sped after her, flashing his lights on and off to get her attention. She only increased her speed.

He pressed the accelerator. Maybe then she'd notice him. Her car increased speed, as well. He edged close enough to see that it was man, not Elizabeth, who was driving.

He stayed close to the car, not bothering to reach for his phone. He could not lose the precious minutes it would take to call for help or risk not being able to maintain a tail.

They drove for miles. Though he could keep the compact car in his sight, he couldn't overtake it on the winding road.

A thought plagued him that maybe Elizabeth

wasn't even in the car. Maybe she was back at the sugar beet factory fighting for her life.

The road straightened out, and he took the opportunity to zoom up beside the car. The man behind the wheel was not Kenny. He looked menacing as he glanced in Zach's direction. He jerked the wheel, clipping Zach's car.

Zach's car swerved off onto a shoulder, but he responded by increasing speed, getting in front of the other car and then slowing down. The little red car sped around him. The sign indicated that the road was about to get curvy again.

The right lane bordered open fields while the left had a slight drop-off. He dared not risk trying to come alongside the car and be run off the road.

All he could do was stay on the guy's bumper and hope he ran out of gas before Zach did.

The guy slammed the brakes on suddenly. Zach rear-ended him. Metal crunched. His body jerked forward. The air bag deployed, and he was flung back. Zach took a moment to reorient himself.

His door flung open and hands grabbed him, pulling him out. Zach glanced at the backseat of Elizabeth's car. She lay motionless in the backseat. The momentary distraction gave the man opportunity to punch Zach in the stomach.

Zach doubled over and fought for air. The man landed a karate chop to the nerve between his neck and shoulder. His body vibrated with pain.

Zach planted his feet and prepared to fight his opponent, despite the pain and the dizziness. He shot his fist across the man's jaw even as he felt himself getting weaker and struggling for air. All the same, he landed blow after blow on the man's body until the man backed off.

He would do whatever it took to help Elizabeth. He changed his strategy and marched toward the car, prepared to drive away with Elizabeth. He swung the car door open. The keys were still in the ignition.

The man had recovered and lunged toward the door, which Zach hadn't closed in his rush to start the engine.

The man leaned in as the car gained speed and twisted the keys free. As soon as the car came to a stop, he pulled Zach out of the seat and kicked him.

Zach fought back, but the other man overpowered him, driving him to the ground. The man grabbed Zach's cell phone out of his pocket and threw it.

"Get up." The man flicked open the trunk of the crumpled back end of the car.

Zach dragged himself to his feet even as black dots filled his vision. The man grabbed him. Zach felt himself slip in and out of consciousness as the man pushed him into the trunk of the car.

Elizabeth came to in a dark room. Her hands were tied behind her, and she was lying on her side. Something about where she was felt and smelled familiar, but it took her a moment to figure out where she was. Her breath caught and her heart fluttered.

She was back inside the main room of Kenny Davis's trailer. Craig must have been paying Kenny to torment her. That explained some of the mixed messages. Kenny's obsession with her made him the perfect candidate. But why had Craig come back to torment her after all these years?

She shuddered. Seeing Craig again had set her back ten years, just when she was starting to feel stronger.

She pushed herself up into a sitting position. Only her hands were bound. She walked over to the little kitchen area. Bending at the waist, she pulled open a drawer with her teeth and then backed up to it in an attempt to retrieve a knife. Her fingers touched cold metal, but when she felt the object, it was clearly a spoon. She tried again. This time, the sharp blade of a knife grazed her finger. She worked it into her hands with care and then sawed at the rope around her wrists.

Outside the trailer, she heard someone moving around. All the curtains were closed but she caught a flash image of Craig as he passed by. Even glimpsing him made her insides turn to wax.

She couldn't tell what he was doing other than making noise and banging against the flimsy walls of the trailer.

Feeling a sense of urgency, she sawed back and forth until the rope had a little give in it, and she was able to twist free. She pulled back the curtain. Craig had skirted around the trailer. She couldn't see clearly, but he had something in his hand that he set down on the ground.

When she tried the door to the trailer, it was locked. The windows were too small to crawl through. She peered outside again and gasped as flames licked the sides of the trailer. Craig had been spreading gasoline around the base of it.

Panic shot through her as she ran into the little room where Kenny had kept her. Maybe that window would be big enough to escape through. A body lay on the bed. At first she thought the man was dead until she saw his chest expand.

She rolled him over on his back. Zach. He

must have figured something out from the text she'd sent him and come after her. She shook him and called him name. He was unresponsive.

"Oh, Zach, please. Wake up." He didn't move, and she realized that finding a way out for both of them had to be her priority. She could drag him through the window if she had to—but first, she needed to get it open.

She searched around for some sort of tool to detach the plywood. She ran back to the kitchen and found a heavy-duty spoon that she used as a lever between the board and the wall. After sliding the window open, she managed to tear the plywood free just as the trailer filled with smoke. She coughed, then tried again to wake Zach.

She patted his cheek a little harder. This time she got a groan out of him. The smoke grew thicker. She struggled for a deep breath.

Zach coughed, and his eyes fluttered open.

"We need to get out of here…through the window." Her voice faltered.

Zach looked at her, but his expression didn't mirror the level of panic she felt. He still wasn't coherent.

She gripped his shoulders and physically turned him. "This way."

Though he moved slowly, he seemed to finally comprehend what she was telling him. He pushed himself through the window, landing feet first. When she peered out the window, the heat from the flames made her hesitate.

"Jump clear of it, Elizabeth." Zach's voice sounded stronger.

She pushed herself off the sill, but felt a burning sensation on her leg. When she whirled around, her pant leg had caught fire. Zach stomped on the pant leg and beat down the flames with his hand.

"Are you hurt?"

She sucked in air through her teeth. "It stings a little."

The flames continued to consume the trailer. He pulled her farther away from the intense heat. Her little compact car was gone, as was Kenny's truck. They were in a remote enough area that it might be hours before anyone saw the smoke and called emergency services—if the fire was spotted at all.

Zach tugged on her sleeve. "Let's head down the road."

As they ran, the pain from the burn on her leg intensified. It could be hours before they encountered anyone. She favored her foot. Zach turned back.

"It's bothering you, isn't it?"

"A little, but I can keep going." Craig couldn't have gone far. He would be after them.

He shook his head. "This way." He led her down the embankment to a stream. He pulled her shoe off and then tore away some of the burned fabric with his hands.

He lifted her foot and placed it in the stream. The river water was almost icy but soothing all the same.

He pulled her foot out of the water. "Better?"

She nodded.

"Kenny got released today through some legal snafu," Zach said.

"It wasn't Kenny who took me this time." The words seemed to freeze in her throat. "For some reason, Craig Miller was behind all this."

"Oh, Elizabeth." He touched her cheek tenderly. And then his voice filled with rage. "We're going to get him."

She just wanted to get away from Craig. On the road above them, Elizabeth's compact car appeared. A man got out and peered down at them. He had a gun in his hand. It had to be Craig.

Zach lifted Elizabeth up by the shoulders. They splashed through the stream and out into a grassy area. Craig made his way down the bank and raced after them. Elizabeth was slowed by her injury and Zach stayed with her, wrapping an arm around her waist and trying to support her. They ran along the river until if opened up into a reservoir.

"Can you swim?"

She answered him by diving in. The cold water paralyzed her for a moment before her hand sliced through the current. She could hear Zach splashing beside her. They swam until they came to a rock outcropping. She rested her arms on the rock while her feet still dangled in the water. Craig had not followed them into the lake. Instead he skirted the edges. But he didn't shoot at them.

Zach pointed at the opposite side of the lake. "That way. He won't be able to get around fast enough."

She pushed off the rock and stroked through the water. After ten minutes, they both stopped to tread water and catch their breath.

Craig had disappeared from view, but she was sure he hadn't given up. As bent on killing her as he was, she knew he would find another way to get at them.

SEVENTEEN

Though it was summertime, Zach was shivering by the time they dragged themselves onto the rocky shore of the lake. Both of them lay on their stomachs, gasping for breath.

After a long moment, he rose to his feet and glanced around. He couldn't see Craig Miller anywhere. That didn't mean they were safe. Craig had seen where they were headed. The road ran parallel with part of the lake. Maybe he'd gone back for Elizabeth's car and was waiting for them to reconnect with the road.

"Let's follow the road without getting on the road," he said. "He'll be looking for us there."

His soaked clothes hung heavily on his frame. They headed up a hill until they came close to the road. Zach checked where the sun was in the sky. It had been behind them when they'd run from the trailer. Now it was close to dark. "This way," he said.

He could see the road above them as they crouched low.

He heard the sound of a car engine. Both of them dove into the tall grass. Elizabeth's car eased by them. Craig must be patrolling the road looking for them. It was a risk to stay this close to the road, but the greater risk would be getting lost in the forest.

They stayed low, shielded by the tall grass as they ran. When Zach looked over his shoulder, he could see the smoke rising up from where the burning trailer was. Would anyone spot it and be alarmed?

He saw a flash of movement in his peripheral vision. Craig was running toward them at a rapid pace. Zach grabbed Elizabeth's hand and veered back into the trees.

Elizabeth still lagged behind. Her foot caught on a log and she fell. He ran back to help her up.

"Are you okay, can you run?"

She nodded, but he could tell by the look on her face that she was in pain from the burn.

They stumbled forward. Something hit the back of his shoulder, a stinging pain radiated down his arm. It took him a moment to comprehend that he'd been hit with a tranquilizer.

He could feel the strength leaving his body. He fell to his knees. Elizabeth tried to pull him up, but he wobbled on his feet. Elizabeth yanked the tranquilizer dart out of his shoulder.

Though his vision blurred, he saw Craig step into the clearing and aim the gun at Elizabeth.

Elizabeth awoke tied to a tree. Craig Miller sat on the other side of the fire he'd built.

He threw another log on the flames. "Pretty good fire for a city guy, huh?"

She swallowed hard trying to form words, struggling to find a response. Terror made her stomach clench tight. She turned her head one way and then the other, not seeing Zach anywhere.

"Too bad the two of you didn't die in that trailer. That would have been the perfect story. So tidy," Craig said.

She wondered if Craig had already killed Zach. She suppressed the despair the thought created and cleared her throat. "The perfect story?"

Craig poked the fire with a stick. "I had a local lawyer get Kenny released. The way it would have looked, my dear, is that Kenny killed the two of you in a fit of jealous rage. After he set the camper on fire, he took his truck and drove it into the lake. Murder-suicide. A classic."

Blood froze in her veins. Kenny was dead. Craig had killed him.

She knew Craig wouldn't be explaining things to her unless he intended to kill her, as well. "Why are you here, after all this time?"

He jabbed at the fire some more. "They are still putting the case together, but you would have received a call from a lawyer in Seattle, maybe in a few weeks or so. I'm not supposed to know about it, of course, but it helps that I'm an attorney and privy to lots of gossip." He pulled the stick out of the fire. It glowed orange at the end. "Always good to get the jump on things."

She shook her head. "The statute ran out for me to get any justice for what you did to me."

Craig raised an eyebrow. "For *you*."

All the air left her lungs and she shuddered. She could put the puzzle pieces together. Craig must have attacked another woman. So she was probably going to be called as a witness to establish a pattern of behavior. She fought against her mind going cloudy. She'd found the strength to face Kenny's tormenting. She wanted to believe that Craig no longer had power over her either. But the vibrations that started in her spine and worked their way through her limbs told her he still had a hold on her mind.

She wiggled a little to test how tightly the

rope was wound around her. She had very little room to move.

Craig said, "I came out here to let you know all the legal ways I could destroy you if you chose to testify. Instead I ran into your number one obsessed fan, who was more than willing to help me out for a little money and the promise of being with you. Then I made a call to that other newscaster, so he could mess with your mind. I didn't even have to get my hands dirty."

"You thought you could rattle me enough through Kenny, so I would fall apart again like I did last time." Now she understood why Kenny hadn't initially tried to kill her. But now, killing her was clearly on the table.

"Nobody had to die. You just needed to be so shredded you would make a bad witness just like before." Craig rose to his feet, broke the stick he'd been holding over his knee and tossed it in the fire. "But now you and your boyfriend have gone and ruined everything."

"Where is Zach?"

He waggled a finger at her. "Always the curious little reporter." Craig paced. "As it is, I'm going to have to make this all look like an accident."

That must be why he didn't want to use the gun. "The police will figure it out."

"I've covered my tracks. As a lawyer, it's

amazing what you can learn from the criminals you represent." He pulled a knife out of his pocket and cut the ropes that bound her. "Pick up the ropes. We don't want to leave any evidence that we were ever here."

She gathered the ropes in her hands.

When she straightened, he grabbed her at the elbow and yanked her. She pulled away as deep terror ignited inside her.

"Still a little jumpy." Craig grabbed her again.

The fear she felt when he touched her nearly paralyzed her. Her stomach coiled into tight knots. "I'm just fine." The falter in her voice suggested otherwise.

Craig leaned close, his voice filled with menace. "Still as pretty as ever, Elizabeth. Too bad things didn't work out between us." His hot breath burned her cheek.

She pulled free of his grasp. Rage like she had never felt before overtook her. She slapped Craig in the face.

His eyes grew round with anger. He clamped his hands around her wrist. She tried to twist away. He grabbed the other wrist, as well.

He pulled her toward his chest. "Such a pretty woman, but foolish."

Terror and rage wrestled within her. Something told her that it was the rage that would save her. She kicked him hard in the shin.

He yowled and let go of her. She turned and darted toward the trees, heart beating wildly. Feet pounding. She sprinted, willing her feet to move faster.

She felt the weight of Craig's body on her back as he tackled her. He bent her arm behind her at an unnatural angle. "You dare to run away from me."

She clenched her teeth against the pain he caused. No way would she give him the satisfaction of hearing her cry out.

He took his knee off her back. "Turn over," he commanded. He pushed on her arm until the pain radiated up to her shoulder. "I said turn over."

She twisted slightly, and he let go of her arm.

He offered her a menacing grin. "There's my pretty lady." His expression hardened. "Don't try that again. Understand?"

Some deep survival instinct told her not to fight back…just yet. She simply nodded.

He reached out and touched her cheek. She jerked back as the terror returned tenfold. Would he have this control over her for the rest of her life? Not if she could tap into the anger she'd felt. No woman deserved what he'd done to her.

She stood up and he rose to stop her from running.

More than anything she wanted Craig Miller

to go to jail. If not for what he'd done to her, then for the other woman he'd destroyed.

He made a tsk tsk noise. "Poor little scared Elizabeth." His voice dripped with sarcasm.

"You can't keep doing this to women."

He lunged at her and she jumped. "Can't I?"

She hated that the fear had won again. All the same, she planted her feet and lifted her chin even though her stomach felt like it was doing somersaults.

He leaned close to her. His proximity made her tremble. "The car is just up on the road. Don't try anything, or I'll make you hurt before you die." He pushed on her back. "Go now."

She marched through the trees toward the road. Her red car stood out from all the green and browns of the forest. Without moving her head much, she searched the area for any sign of Zach.

Craig opened the driver's-side door and pulled out a roll of duct tape. "Hold out your hands."

She hesitated. Was there a way to escape? Once she was in the car and bound, it would be almost impossible.

"I said hold out your hands."

She lifted her hands, palms together even as she looked around, hating the feel of his hands on hers as he applied the tape. If she ran, he'd just catch her again. He opened the back door and shoved her in, then got into the driver's seat.

She glanced around the backseat. There was nothing she could use to hit him with.

"I've been thinking we can still work this into a murder-suicide angle." He spoke casually as though he were relaying the plot for a television show. "There's no reason why there can't be two cars in that lake."

His words were like a blow to her face. How was she going to get out of here before he drowned her? Where was Zach? Her heart seized up. She feared the worst, that Craig had already killed him.

From the trunk where he'd been imprisoned once again, Zach felt the car start to move. Tires rolled along in the dirt. Craig must have lifted him into the trunk once the tranquilizer took effect. He'd been in such a hurry he hadn't tied Zach up.

The car picked up speed as Zach felt around the interior of the trunk. His fingers touched hard metal, a crowbar and a jack. Elizabeth's car had an armrest in the backseat that folded up to create part of the seat. He pushed on it, feeling resistance. Weight must be resting against it. He punched it hard several times. A moment later, it opened.

Light streamed into the trunk. He had a view of the back of the front seat. He pressed his face closer to the opening. He could see Elizabeth's torso and her bound hands. His hands were free but he was trapped in the trunk.

Craig was probably watching her closely in the rearview mirror. She was smart enough not to look through the opening. He felt around for the crowbar and angled his body in the tiny space so he could shove it through the opening. He set it on the armrest. She gave him a thumbs up with her bound hands but didn't move the rest of her body.

The car continued to roll down the road. It slowed and then they were traveling downhill. Elizabeth had the crowbar. He felt around for the jack. It was at his feet. He couldn't reach it with his hands in the confined space. He pushed it up toward his hands with his foot. His fingertips just touched it. He scrunched his body closer toward it.

The car slowed down even more. The guy was going to stop at any second. An inch more and he'd have a grip on the jack.

If Craig saw the crowbar, he'd know something was up. Hopefully Elizabeth had enough freedom of movement to hide it from view. She wouldn't be very effective at swinging it with her hands tied together, but they needed to use everything they had to fight back.

The car came to a stop. They had seconds before they were discovered. He could touch the cold metal of the jack but not grip it yet. His feet pressed against the wall of the trunk. If he could just stretch his hand an inch more or bend his upper body in the tiny space...

He could hear most of the conversation through the open armrest.

"Yes," said Craig. "I think this spot will do quite nicely." His door opened and slammed shut.

"Craig, please think about this." Elizabeth's voice faltered. "Do you want to go to jail for rape and murder?"

"The thing is, my dear Elizabeth, I'm not going to get caught for either."

Zach's whole body stiffened. The arrogance in Craig Miller's voice fueled his rage and desire for justice.

"They'll figure out that Kenny died first," Elizabeth sounded frantic.

"Forensics doesn't work well for bodies found underwater...if they are ever even found."

The car door opened. Elizabeth closed the armrest, and the trunk went dark again. Zach stretched his hand willing his fingers to be longer. He compressed his body so his hand would be closer to the jack. His fingers wrapped around the metal. He pulled the jack up toward his chest.

When Craig opened the trunk, he'd be ready to spring on him. The car shook as though someone was moving around. A door slammed. Feet crunched on gravel. One set or two sets? He couldn't tell.

Several minutes passed. He tensed, ready to spring as soon as the trunk swung open. The muffled sound of Craig's voice reached his ears.

The armrest came open. Elizabeth poked her head in revealing that she was gagged. She tilted her head toward the front of the car, maybe indicating that was where Craig had gone.

She craned her neck. When she looked back at him, her eyes had gone wide with fear. She fumbled to close the armrest. The car shook and a door opened, then closed.

Zach gripped the jack and waited. The seconds seemed to last an hour each. Several times, something banged against the car and then the car door slammed. He waited, wondering what had just taken place. Maybe Craig wasn't even going to get him out of the trunk. What exactly did the man have in mind if he was making it look like Kenny had murdered them?

More footsteps. The trunk clicked open. Zach was momentarily paralyzed by the flood of light to his eyes. Craig reached for the jack. Zach sat upright and pushed the jack hard against Craig's chest, causing him to take a step back.

Seeing Craig made Zach's anger shift into overdrive. This was the man who had ruined Elizabeth's life and made it impossible for her to trust. He jumped to his feet still standing in the trunk. He threw the jack at Craig and leaped on him. He punched Craig over and over.

The sound of a car rolling forward drew his attention. The car must have been in Neutral. Now he saw that Elizabeth was behind the wheel—likely unconscious or tied in place, otherwise she would have escaped. He jumped off Craig and ran after the car as it headed toward the deep waters of the lake.

The car picked up speed rolling downhill. Zach reached out for the handle of the driver's-side door just as the front end of the car hit the water. The door swung open. It took only seconds before the whole car was in the lake and sinking. He dove underwater. His arms reached out for Elizabeth, but he couldn't see clearly. The entire car was submerged. He grabbed hold of her, clawing at the tape that bound her to the steering wheel until he pulled her free. They swam to the surface.

His head burst through the water. He gasped for air. Holding Elizabeth, he swam away from where Craig lay on the ground, immobilized from the pummeling Zach had given him. He dragged Elizabeth to a sandbar. Craig turned over on his side and pushed himself to his feet.

Elizabeth sputtered and opened her eyes.

Zach glanced over his shoulder. Though he swayed once he was on his feet, Craig made his way toward them.

"Can you get up?" Zach whispered to Elizabeth.

She nodded.

He reached out a hand pulling her to her feet. Craig had recovered enough that he was trotting toward them.

Elizabeth was still impeded by the burn on her leg. Nearly drowning had probably stolen some of her strength, too. But she stood tall at his side, clearly determined not to back down.

It was two against one. He wasn't sure what Craig was thinking.

Craig drew close to them and slowed down. He pulled a gun from his jacket pocket.

The first shot nipped at their heels as they turned to run. This was not the tranquilizer gun he'd used before. Maybe Craig had given up on making their deaths look like an accident. It meant he was getting desperate. They ran through the trees and up to the road. When Zach looked over his shoulder, he didn't see Craig. That didn't mean they were in the clear.

They ran, not sure where they were headed. The road turned into a two track. As they rounded a curve, the gray, slanted buildings of a ghost town came into view. Most of the edifices were falling down, roofs caved in. Another gunshot cracked the air around them. Zach still couldn't see Craig. The shot had come from the tree line above them. He pulled Elizabeth in the opposite direction toward a cabin with a sod roof. They slipped around the back of the cabin.

Both of them pressed against the weathered wood, breathing heavily. Zach pointed to a barnlike structure. The cabin would obstruct Craig's view, so he wouldn't know which building they'd run into next.

They burst across the overgrown grass and dashed into the creaking structure.

"There has to be a back way out." He turned slightly, seeing a flash of movement through the glassless window. Craig had made his way into the ghost town and was probably searching all the buildings near the sod roof cabin.

They had only a few minutes on him.

She ran through the structure to a second room. She turned to him, shaking her head.

"Up to the loft." He was already at the ladder, which did not look that sturdy.

"We'll be trapped."

"Lofts usually have an opening for tossing out hay bales." Zach said. He hoped he was right. He grabbed a sturdy stick just in case they had to fight Craig off.

She hurried up the ladder. One of the rungs snapped, but she didn't cry out. He saw another flash of movement. Craig was getting closer.

He made his way up the ladder. Another rung broke, this one causing him to slip down. She reached out her hand to him, pulling him up so he could grasp the edge of the loft and hoist himself up the rest of the way.

They hurried toward the loft opening. The first shot must have come from outside the barn. It hit a wall not too far from them.

It was a bit of a leap from the loft opening to the hard dirt. Both of them landed on their feet and took off running. More gunshots came as they made their way toward a rocky outcropping.

They zigzagged through the labyrinth of rocks up the hillside. Craig fired off several shots. Rocks cascaded over each other.

They sprinted as the rocks thinned out. Zach felt a sting through his shoulder. He knew he'd been hit. Adrenaline masked much of the pain, but the bullet would debilitate him in a matter of minutes.

They were in the middle of nowhere. There was no way to call for help. How were they ever going to get out of this alive?

EIGHTEEN

Elizabeth slowed as Zach lagged behind her. She turned to face him. Even in the dusky light, she could see that his face was whiter than rice.

She shook her head, wondering what was going on.

He gasped for air. "It's nothing. Let's keep going."

Her hand fluttered to her mouth when she saw the bloodstain on his shoulder. "You've been shot."

"It just a nick. I'll be fine." He took off running ahead of her but quickly slowed down.

She came up beside him and placed his arm over her shoulders.

"We can't outrun him. We've got to find a place to hide." She could tell that Zach was growing weaker by the second. He leaned over more as they made their way through the thick brush.

She recognized the cluster of tall trees that

grew along the creek bed. "We're not far from the trailer."

"It'll be burned out." Zach's voice filled with anguish.

"It was metal. Maybe it didn't burn to the ground. There might be something around there we can use."

She wrapped her arm around his waist and held him up. When she craned her neck, Craig was nowhere in sight. They had gotten enough of a lead that Craig would have to spend valuable time trying to figure out which way they'd gone.

Zach leaned against her even more. "Okay, I guess the trailer is our best option."

The trees gave way to open ground, and she saw the smoldering trailer in the distance. As she had predicted, it was only partially burned. As they approached, she directed Zach to a lawn chair by a fire pit.

The knob of the trailer door was still hot to the touch. She grabbed leaves to wrap around it, but found that it was still locked.

Zach slumped in the chair. She ran around to the window where they'd escaped. She grabbed a second lawn chair and hoisted herself up. The entire trailer smelled of smoke and burnt plastic. She coughed. The kitchen area was pretty blackened.

Some years ago, she'd done a story on treating a gunshot wound after a hunter had accidently been shot by his hunting partner. If the bullet was lodged in his skin, it could come out later. The most important thing was to stop the bleeding and keep Zach from going into shock. She found a clean washcloth and some antiseptic in the tiny bathroom.

The upper kitchen cupboards were largely untouched by the fire. She grabbed some food and a sharp knife and stuffed it all into her pockets before climbing back out the window. Zach was conscious, though he was still very pale.

She cut away the cloth around the bloody area.

Zach angled his neck. "The bullet isn't too deep."

She knew about bullet wounds in theory. He knew about them in practice. "That's good, I suppose." She placed the washcloth where the blood flowed, applying pressure.

Zach winced.

"Sorry," she said. "Let's hide out in those trees so you can rest." She held out a hand for him to take. "Can you use your hand to keep pressure on the wound?"

He nodded, sucking in air through his teeth. Anxiety pummeled her thoughts. She had a feeling he was in way more pain than he was letting on. She led him back through the trees until they were some distance from the trailer though she had a view of it.

Zach slumped to the ground. Elizabeth gathered some tree boughs and helped him lay down.

"Rest for a while." She ripped open the package of crackers she'd found and handed him a few. "Eat. It will help you get your strength up."

As night came on, she kept vigil watching for Craig.

It looked like the trailer fire may have burned out before it was noticed. That meant no one was coming, and they were on their own to get off the mountain alive.

As the sky grew darker, she heard Zach's breathing deepen. He'd fallen asleep. She wondered how long they dared to wait before moving again. Sooner or later by process of elimination, Craig would figure out which way they'd gone, but Zach needed to get his strength back.

She watched the shadows as the sky turned from gray to charcoal. With the cover of night, maybe they had a fighting chance.

She heard a noise off to the side of her somewhere in the trees. Zach sat up, as well. Though she could not see clearly, she thought she saw a dark figure moving toward the trailer. Then a small light came on. The kind of flashlight that was on a cell phone.

Zach leaned close to her ear and whispered. "We should go."

They circled back through the trees, and came out on the road when they were out of view of the trailer. Craig would expect them to follow the road…but the other option was getting lost in the woods. She only hoped they had enough of a head start to avoid another run-in with Craig and his gun. They were both injured and moving slowly. This time, they might not survive.

As much as possible, they used the trees and brush close to the road as cover. The darkness and the need to step carefully slowed them down. Zach stopped to rest, leaning against a tree and looking out on the road.

The effort at moving clearly was draining him of strength. "How is the shoulder?"

"It hurts and I can't lift my arm very high."

If Zach was willing to admit that much, then the pain must be horrible. He needed medical attention and soon. It was at least an hour's drive up the mountain to Kenny's trailer. How long would it take them to walk it?

She heard the sound of a car engine approaching.

"I can't tell if the car is coming up the mountain or down."

Zach tugged on her shirt and pulled her back toward the trees. "Let's just watch."

Headlights came into view headed up the mountain.

They jumped out on the road and waved the car down. The car sped past but stopped at twenty feet up the road.

She ran toward the car. The man rolled down the window.

"What on earth," he said.

She couldn't see the man's face clearly. "Please, my friend has been shot. We could use your help. I know you're headed up the mountain, but would you mind turning around?"

"No problem, hop in. I'll take you down. A friend in need and all that."

She ran to the edge of the road and waved Zach over. Zach stumbled out of the trees as the man got turned around, then both of them piled into the backseat.

Elizabeth took in a breath and stared at the back of the man's head. "So why were you headed up the mountain at this hour?"

"A neighbor at the base of the mountain reported seeing a fire earlier. Thought I'd go up and check it out."

"At this hour?" said Zach, his voice laced with suspicion.

"Had a busy day. This is the first chance I had to get away."

She understood Zach's suspicion. Craig had already enlisted one man to help him. What if he had others?

Her heart fluttered a little as she tried to remember if she'd even seen any houses at the base of the mountain.

Zach leaned against Elizabeth. "Where do you work?" His voice sounded a little weak though she could tell he'd slipped into reporter mode.

"I'm a sculptor. I work from home. But this far out of town we try to look out for each other. I know Kenny Davis was a strange man, but he is still my neighbor." The man drove along in silence for a long moment. "I don't suppose you saw him up there."

Elizabeth wasn't sure how to respond to the question. Kenny and his truck were at the bottom of the lake.

"His story was all over the news." The man did a double take in the rearview mirror. "As a matter of fact…"

A weariness crept over Elizabeth. "Yes, I'm the woman he kidnapped."

"How about that. Elizabeth Kramer is in my

car." She caught a flash of the man's grin in the mirror, and all her suspicions washed away.

"I know you probably have a lot of questions. I really appreciate you helping us, so I don't want to seem rude, but we just need to get to a safe place where we can call the police. Do you have a cell phone?"

"I never remember to bring it with me. I'm Roy, by the way."

A dark figure jumped out on the road. Roy swerved to avoid him, sending the car sailing toward the ditch.

Roy's body swung forward and then back as the front end of the car hit the ditch. He wasn't moving. Elizabeth scrambled to orient herself. The driver's-side door swung open. Craig grabbed the barely conscious Roy and dragged him out of the driver's seat.

He slipped behind the wheel and backed the car out of the ditch, leaving Roy lying on the ground as they headed back up the mountain.

Zach rested his head against Elizabeth's shoulder. He was conscious but barely. She stared at the back of Craig's head, rage simmering inside her.

"That man probably saw you," said Elizabeth.

"I doubt it. It was dark."

"What are you going to do?"

"I'm sure there are places up in these hills where a body can never be found. We just need to find some remote, faraway spot."

So that was his new plan. Elizabeth's mind raced a hundred miles an hour. There must be some way to rattle Craig. "They'll trace the gun to you."

Craig laughed. "I told you. I know all the tricks of the trade. Working with criminals does have its perks."

Craig hadn't had time to tie her up, but attacking him while he was driving with the steep drop off on the side of the road was too risky. She leaned forward in the seat. Once they got to a place where he could shoot them, their options would narrow.

The road became rougher as the car bounced up and down. Craig stopped the car. "I need to keep an eye on you." He turned to face her. "Get up front and drive."

Zach raised his head and looked at her. Her heart squeezed tight over the warmth she saw there, despite the pain he must be in.

"Quit making doe eyes at him and get up front." Craig spat out his words.

Zach nodded and brushed her hand lightly. She wondered if he had some sort of plan. Even if he did, was he even strong enough to execute it?

"Hurry up." Craig grew more angry by the moment.

The affection Zach had displayed for her seemed to upset Craig.

She pushed open the door and got into the driver's side of the car. Craig sat in the passenger seat. He aimed the gun at Zach. "Don't try anything funny or your boyfriend gets it."

Elizabeth bit back the rising terror. She needed to stay strong and focused, for herself and for Zach. She pressed the accelerator leaning forward to see more clearly in the dark.

The car jerked along on the bumpy road.

"He is your boyfriend, isn't he?" Envy colored every word Craig spoke.

She bit back the bitterness and the pain the question brought to the surface. "I wish he could be." She kept her voice level, not giving away how upset she was. She wasn't about to let Craig see her weakening.

"You *wish* he could be?" Craig's voice dripped with sarcasm. "Poor Ice Princess Elizabeth. You and I could have had something if it hadn't been for that *misunderstanding*."

She gripped the steering wheel so tight her fingers hurt.

He leaned close to her. "We still could have

that." His finger snaked down her cheek. "You want that, don't you?"

She jerked away.

A voice boomed from the back seat, "Get your hands off her."

Zach leaned forward and punched Craig across the jaw. Craig turned his gun on Zach.

Elizabeth slammed on the brakes, causing Craig to lurch forward and back in the seat. But he recovered quickly and aimed the gun at Zach, his finger on the trigger. Elizabeth lunged toward him but her seat belt held her in place. The gun went off.

She unclicked her seat belt and hit Craig with both fists.

Craig poked the gun in Elizabeth's belly. "Just try it."

She pulled back. Rage still boiled inside her. She clenched her teeth. She gave a side-long glance to Zach, whose face was twisted in agony. He clutched his arm. She took in a breath that felt like it had broken glass in it. Had Zach been shot again?

Zach locked her in his gaze. His eyes were glazed with pain, but his voice was steady and strong. "It's going to be all right."

Craig stabbed her in the side with the gun barrel. "Drive."

Her hands were shaking as she turned the key

in the ignition and pressed the gas. Her throat was tight with fear and worry. She needed to know if Zach had been shot again.

"Please, Craig, I beg of you. Can we stop the car and make sure Zach is okay?"

"What does it matter if he dies in the car or dies deep in the mountains?" He poked the gun in her shoulder. "Keep driving."

She heard a groan from the backseat. Was that Zach trying to tell her he was okay or was the pain so unbearable he had to cry out?

As the road became rougher, she slowed the car down. "How are you going to get out of here? They'll know this car was stolen."

"I've already hidden two cars and one body. I have a cell phone and a man with a helicopter who owes me a favor. In a matter of hours, I'll be back in Seattle, sitting at my desk, ready to attend a party for me making partner in my law firm. That's how it works, Elizabeth. I win. I always win."

The rage that simmered inside her started to boil. She knew she needed to keep it under control and wait for the right moment. Craig Miller was not getting away with this again. There had to be some justice in this world. Then she noticed Craig still had not clipped into his seat belt after aiming the gun at Zach.

Craig leaned forward. "This looks like the

end of the earth here. Stop the car and get out. Get that loser boyfriend of yours out of the car, as well."

The anger inside her exploded. She pressed the accelerator to the floor.

"What are you doing?" Craig gripped the armrest.

The car crashed down the hill through brush and over small trees as it lurched and lunged. She kept her feet on the gas as a large tree loomed in front of her. She braced for impact.

Metal crumpled. Craig screamed. The car was an older model without air bags. The car body seemed to vibrate for a long moment after impact. She opened her eyes. Craig rested his head against the window. She could see that he was still breathing.

It had been a calculated risk to crash the car. Aside from some bruising, the seat belt had saved her. She pushed open the door and hurried to the backseat.

Zach still looked very pale. He smiled at her. "Good job."

She reached over and unclicked his seat belt. "Can you move?" Zach still held his hand over his bloodstained forearm.

"It's just a graze."

She wondered if he was lying to keep her from worrying.

Zach slid across the seat and placed his feet on the ground. "We should get his gun."

In the front seat, Craig groaned.

She leaned forward and scanned the floor of the car, not seeing the gun anywhere. It must be under Craig's body.

Craig stirred and lifted his head. They needed to get away before he could shoot them.

"Too risky. No time. Let's get out of here." She wrapped her arm around Zach's waist. The mountain was steep. Making it back up to the road was slow going.

Craig tumbled out of the car still not completely coherent. They both increased their pace. Her legs strained on the steep hill. Zach broke free from her and tried to stand on his own. From the way he bent over, he was very weak.

Craig was still stumbling around. They had precious few minutes before they would be used for target practice again.

NINETEEN

Zach could feel himself losing strength by the minute from the blood loss. But for Elizabeth's sake, he wasn't going to give up the fight that easily.

He glanced down the mountain. Though he couldn't see clearly, it looked like Craig was making his way up to them.

He directed Elizabeth toward some brush. Crouching caused pain to slice across his shoulder. He swallowed a groan.

He could hear Craig moving in the brush behind them, gaining on them.

He stepped close to Elizabeth and whispered, "I'm slowing you down. Go without me."

She shook her head adamantly. "We're in this together."

They pushed through the brush. From the sound of it, Craig was parallel to them but unable to find them in the darkness and thick undergrowth. They pressed close together, not moving. Craig may be somewhat debilitated from the accident, but the gun and their injuries gave him too much of an advantage.

Craig's footsteps drew farther away. Chances were he'd double back in minutes. They needed to come up with a plan that didn't involve them having to outrun him. Neither of them had the strength to do that.

He waited until Craig's footsteps faded completely. He touched Elizabeth lightly on the elbow and directed her back down the hill.

"Back to the car," he whispered. It was a huge risk. Would the car even start? Would they be able to navigate the incline?

The first gunshot flared behind them when they were halfway down the hill. He could see the metal gleam of the car in the moonlight. Each step on the incline caused pain to charge through him. They reached the car. It didn't look like it was too tightly wedged against the tree. Both doors were still open. He jumped into the driver's side. Elizabeth had left the key in the ignition.

The engine churned but didn't start. Elizabeth craned her neck. "I can't see where he is." Panic filled her voice.

Another shot boomed. This one shattered the back windshield. Elizabeth bent forward. He tried the key again. This time it fired to life.

Elizabeth clicked her seat belt into place and then reached over and did the same for him.

"It saved your life once," she said.

He shifted into Reverse and pressed the gas. The metal of the car body creaked and groaned. He met with resistance at first, but managed to back it away from the tree. He turned the wheel sharply.

Elizabeth screamed. Craig appeared at the passenger window, which was partially rolled down. He reached in and grabbed at Elizabeth. He must be out of bullets if he was trying the up-close-and-personal approach.

"I'll get you," Craig yelled. His words dripped venomous hate.

Elizabeth leaned toward Zach, seeking to get away from Craig's grasp. Sheer terror etched across her features. Craig stepped away from the car as it picked up speed.

Zach focused on the steep terrain, swerving to avoid the larger trees and rocks that would make them crash again. The car bumped over smaller logs and brush. The incline grew steeper. Elizabeth pressed her back against the seat and gripped the armrest.

The car caught air and landed with a jolt. The engine seized. White-hot pain vibrated across his shoulder and arm.

He leaned forward and turned the key in

the ignition. This time, it sputtered and died. They'd landed on a steep incline with the front end of the car facing down. The car eased forward. Metal crunched and bent.

He fumbled for his seat belt. "Bail."

He pushed open the door and tumbled out as the car slid down the mountain. They heard the crash and crumpling of metal somewhere in the distance below them. As the dust cleared, he caught a glimpse of Elizabeth sitting, bracing her hands behind her.

He rose to his feet with some effort and groaning.

She looked up at him. "Good timing there, Zach."

He appreciated that she could find humor at a moment like this. He reached out a hand to her.

"I can get up on my own. You look like you can barely stand." Her voice was filled with concern.

Even if they'd managed to shake Craig, they had a long way to go before they were safe.

They walked down the remainder of the hillside until it leveled off. He knew it was up to them to find their way back to civilization. He moved slower every minute they were out here. They didn't have much time.

Elizabeth must have picked up on something in his posture because she hurried over to him and slipped under his arm to offer support. They stumbled along what looked like an old logging road.

In the distance, they heard the sound of a helicopter. He couldn't see anything in the night sky. It could be rescue, and or it could be Craig getting picked up by his friend.

"We should probably seek some cover," he said. "Until it's clear if that is a friend or foe."

They wandered toward some trees. If it was Craig, would he try to save himself and get out of here without trying to find them again? The more likely scenario was that he would make sure they were both dead and then leave. Having witnesses would be his undoing, even if he could manage to escape.

Zach's knees buckled just as they entered the cover of some trees.

Elizabeth collapsed on the ground beside him. Her voice filled with worry. "You need medical attention."

The helicopter noise grew louder.

"Elizabeth, save yourself. You're better off going without me."

"I won't leave you." She touched his cheek.

He pulled her hand away. "There is no reason we both have to die. You can get back and tell them what Craig has done."

The helicopter grew louder. Though the trees

provided cover for them, it sounded like the chopper was directly above them.

"Hide over there in that brush," she said.

"Good, you're going to save yourself," he said.

She helped him make his way to the hiding spot.

She leaned close to his ear. "No, I'm going to create a distraction, so we both can get out of here."

Elizabeth raced through the forest, getting far enough away from Zach so she wouldn't give away his location. Then she burst out from the trees. The chopper was low to the ground. The dark color told her it wasn't a rescue chopper.

She waited until the chopper turned, spotting her, before she took off running. She wove in and out of the trees so she'd disappear and then come back into view. The chopper kept up with her.

The force of its blades created a windstorm around her. If she could lead them far enough away and then lose them, she might be able to circle back for Zach.

She came out into an open area. The chopper was loud at her back. The first rifle shot caused her to stutter in her steps. She recovered quickly and sprinted ahead, running in a zig-zag pattern to avoid being an easy target. The undergrowth was thick up ahead. If she could make it there, she'd be shielded. They would have to get out on foot to find her.

She was thirty yards from the thick under-growth when another shot whizzed past her. She dove to the ground and crawled.

A bright light shone on her. She rolled to one side and edged toward the tall grass. The searchlight swept past her as the helicopter landed in the open meadow. From her vantage point, she saw one man get out. The bright light made it impossible for her to tell if it was Craig or not.

She waited until the spotlight swept in the other direction and then crawled into the deeper brush. She pushed herself to her feet and re-sumed running. She didn't hear noises behind her. Maybe she'd shaken her pursuer. Her run slowed to a trot. Her own footsteps seemed al-most too loud. Her heart raged inside her chest, and she ached all over, especially her injured foot. She slowed down even more, listening for approaching footsteps.

The silence was even more frightening than the sound of someone hot on her heels. She wondered what her pursuer had planned. Had she really been able to shake him that easily?

She turned in the general direction of where she'd left Zach. A branch broke behind her. She pressed against a tree, holding her breath. She heard only a single footstep press on the thick, twig-laden forest floor.

After a long moment and no further noise, she pushed herself off the tree and took a tentative step. Her pulse drummed in her ears. The hairs stood up on the back of her head. She sensed someone was close.

Why wasn't he using his flashlight? He must want to ambush her.

She lifted her foot and placed it cautiously on the soft ground. She absorbed all the noise around her but didn't pick up on anything that sounded human. Yet she sensed she was under threat.

She took a few more cautious steps. Once the moonlight provided enough illumination to mark a clear path, she sprinted with all her strength.

Though she still didn't hear anything, she could feel the weight of eyes watching her. She slipped off the obvious path and veered through the thick forest, weaving around trees. Still, she felt the person behind her as if he were breathing down her neck even though he made no noise.

She ran deeper into the forest, knowing she

couldn't return to Zach until she shook this man. She moved as fast as the darkness would allow until she couldn't bring herself to run anymore. Stopping to catch her breath, she listened carefully to the sounds around her.

Trees creaked. She thought she heard footfall that stopped seconds after she quit moving. Anxiety solidified inside her. Was she imagining she was being followed? If the man knew where she was, why didn't he pounce on her? This couldn't be Craig. This man was too stealthy. Anxiety snaked around her rib cage. She was too exhausted to keep up this cat and mouse game.

She rolled herself around the tree so she was on the opposite side of it. Her first step was a careful one to make sure she was quiet and then she darted away. The landscape was nothing more than shadows. She wasn't sure where she was going. Her only thought was that she needed to get away from this man.

She ran until she was out of breath again. Stopping in a clearing, she rested her hands on her knees and sucked in air.

The man pounced on her without warning. His arms were around her instantly, making it impossible to react before her hands were bound in front of her. He tossed her on the ground and disappeared into the trees.

Minutes passed and then Craig appeared.

"Did you like my accomplice? He's a mercenary who got into a little trouble with the law. He won't talk to anyone. He's also a helicopter pilot."

Elizabeth pushed herself up in a sitting position and angled her body away from Craig.

He grabbed her and spun her around. "This is the end for you, Elizabeth. You have discredited and tormented me enough." He touched her cheek and tilted his head, drawing his lips into a pout. "But not before you and I have some fun."

A terror like she had never known invaded every cell of her body.

Please, Lord, not again.

TWENTY

Despite the pain and weakness, Zach raced through the forest. He'd seen where the chopper had come down, which gave him a good idea of where to find Elizabeth. Entering the meadow, he crouched low, using the tree line for cover. The chopper looked abandoned. He strode over to it and peered inside.

He fumbled through a tangle of gear behind the pilot's seat until he found a knife, then he headed back to the forest. A muscular man emerged from the trees. Zach dove to the ground; pain radiated through him. The man strode over to the chopper. He lifted his chin as though alerted to some danger.

Though the tall grass camouflaged Zach, he pressed his body against the earth. His shoulder hurt, and he was in an awkward position with his wounded arm under his stomach. He lifted his head to watch.

The man turned a half circle, clearly scrutinizing each blade of grass. Something about the way the man carried himself and monitored his surroundings said he had military training. Where had Craig dug up this guy?

The man walked the length of the chopper, still looking tense and alert. He must sense that something was amiss even though he wouldn't know the knife was gone until he sorted through the pile of gear.

Zach waited a few minutes more until the man moved to the other side of the chopper. Zach, crawling commando-style, eased toward the tree line. Pain throbbed through his shoulder and arm. His breathing was shallow. He kept moving until he made it to the cover of the trees. He took off through the forest to find Elizabeth. He'd tried to make as little noise as possible but still feared that the man in the chopper would be able to track him.

He broke into a trot, feet pounding the ground. The breath scraping his lungs felt like it had tiny knives in it.

Within a few minutes, he was gasping for air. His side hurt. He leaned against a tree.

Oh, Lord, give me strength. I need to find Elizabeth before it's too late.

He pushed himself off the tree and trod through the dense forest at a slower pace. Craig hadn't been anywhere around the chopper, so he must be looking for Elizabeth, too—if he hadn't caught her already.

As he searched the shadows and listened for any sign that humans were close, he feared he might be too late.

He didn't have the smallest warning when a hand reached out and grabbed the back of his neck.

The voice in the darkness was a gruff one. "Stop right there, partner."

Zach held up both hands. In his weakened state, he was no match for this man.

"No more running. You can kiss your life goodbye."

With his face still very close to hers, Craig scraped a thumb down Elizabeth's cheek. She pressed her lips together and swallowed the scream that shot up her throat. She wasn't about to give him the satisfaction of hearing her cry out.

Find the rage, Elizabeth. Fight back.

He leaned close to her.

Fear flickered past her awareness, but then resolve formed inside her, stronger than hardened steel. Craig Miller was not going to hurt her or any woman ever again.

Her hands were bound in front of her, but her fingers were free. She pretended to relax a little as Craig brushed his cheek over hers and dug his fingers into her shoulder. She reached out toward his stomach and twisted the skin at the same time that she sank her teeth into his shoulder.

Craig recoiled backward. She didn't need to see his eyes to know they were filled with rage.

Before he had time to recover, she swung her bound hands like a hammer against the side of his head and then brought her leg up and kicked him underneath his chin. The move made him fall on his back. She kicked him again and again in the side. He rolled over and curled up in a ball, not looking like he was even going to try to fight back.

In the moment before she took off running, she saw Craig Miller for who he really was. A bully, a pathetic bully, who would never again control her life.

Brushing branches out of the way, she dashed through the trees, trying to orient herself back to where she'd left Zach.

A bright light shone in her face. She stopped in her tracks.

A voice she didn't recognize said, "I think you'd better back it up, sister."

She saw two men in silhouette.

"He has a gun." She recognized Zach's voice. "You should do what he says."

The muscular man pushed Zach toward Elizabeth. His shoulder slammed against her. She could feel his body stiffen against the pain.

"Well, Elizabeth, it looks like you don't win after all." Craig's voice pelted her back like toxic rain.

When she turned to look at him, he swaggered toward them.

"This is the end of the line for you and your boyfriend." Craig's voice filled with bravado once again as if the humiliation of a moment before hadn't even happened. He turned toward the muscular man. "Take care of them."

The man lowered the flashlight. Elizabeth saw a scar across the man's lantern jaw. Tattoos decorated his muscular arms. His eyes were as cold as winter.

Zach pressed closer to her. He was physically shaking from the pain he was in, yet he managed to straighten his spine and square his shoulders.

The big muscular man said, "I brought them to you so *you* could take care of them. That was the deal."

"I'll pay you extra. Whatever the going rate is," Craig said. "I'll meet you back at the helicopter." Then he pressed close to Elizabeth.

Zach stepped in between them.

"It's all right," said Elizabeth. She touched

Zach's shoulder. "He doesn't scare me." And Craig Miller no longer lived inside her head, controlling her life and making it impossible for her to trust or to love.

She and Zach would probably die here tonight, but the victory was hers.

Craig lifted his chin and sneered. "My hands are still clean."

Her rage intensified. It bothered her that there would be no justice for the other woman Craig had destroyed. Knowing him, there had probably been more than one. If only there was a way to see him forced to face what he'd done.

"You won't win, Craig. God will see that justice happens," she said.

"God? God can't touch me." Craig sneered.

Maybe she wouldn't live to see it, but she had to believe Craig could not again get away with hurting another woman.

Craig turned to go. Her anger boiled over, and she jumped on him and hit him over and over. Craig yelped in a very feminine way.

Hands pulled her off him.

Craig had crumpled to his knees.

"Get out of here," said the mercenary to Craig. She heard disdain in the man's voice.

Craig rose to his feet, smoothed his shirt and lifted his chin. He spoke to the mercenary. "The bodies need to be put where they can't be found. Then you will be paid in full." He disappeared into the trees.

The mercenary shifted his gun from one hand to the other. "On your knees. Turn your backs to me."

Elizabeth could not take in a deep breath. Her whole body shook from the intensity of the terror stampeding through her. This was it. She and Zach were going to die out here. At least they would die together.

Zach's mind raced at a hundred miles an hour. Even with Elizabeth's help, he knew he was too weak to overpower the man with the gun.

Elizabeth slipped her hand into Zach's. "I love you. We could have had something together."

"Come on, you two. Get on the ground," barked the mercenary.

Her touch warmed him and gave him hope. He looked closer at the hired assassin's tattoos. "Can you give us just a moment?" requested Zach.

The man threw up his arms.

Zach grabbed both her hands, leaned close and kissed her tenderly. He whispered in her ear, "We *will* have a life together."

He wasn't about to give up on the two of

them. After a silent, fervent prayer, Zach pulled away from Elizabeth and turned to face the man who intended to kill them. He pointed at the man's tattoos, which indicated where he'd served as a soldier in Iraq. "How many tours?"

"Four in the Sandbox." The man's voice was completely neutral and his gaze unwavering.

"I've been in A-stan and Syria as a reporter." If he couldn't outmuscle the man, maybe he could form an alliance with him. The man clearly didn't respect Craig.

The man's posture slackened. "You stay with the troops or back at the posh hotel?"

"Embed is the only way to get the real story."

"He was kidnapped and held hostage," Elizabeth said.

The man stepped back. His rifle went slack at his side.

"The man you're working for raped me ten years ago while I was on a date with him. Now he's done it to another woman," Elizabeth said. "That's why he's doing all this—so I can't testify against him. He's making you commit murder so he can get away with rape without consequences."

The man stared off into the distance for a long moment and then turned back toward them. "I'll fire two shots so he thinks I killed you. I gotta get paid for this job. I'll be out of the country before he figures out what happened. You're on your own to find your way out of here."

Zach nodded and took Elizabeth's hand. They walked deeper into the woods. She jumped as the two shots reverberated through the trees, bullets that were meant for their heads.

Zach slowed in his step. His jaw hardened against the pain.

Even though the mercenary had spared them, he was pretty sure that if they had to walk down the mountain, he wouldn't make it to help alive. He could barely stand up. He'd lost too much blood.

Elizabeth looked right at him. "We have to get on the chopper, don't we?"

Zach raised his head, wanting to protest. Going to the chopper would put her in danger again. If they let Craig leave, at least Elizabeth would be safe. But she didn't wait for his answer.

Elizabeth turned around and headed back toward the man who wanted her dead. Zach trailed behind as dread filled his heart. The odds were not in their favor.

Elizabeth sprinted as the sound of the chopper starting up filled the forest. When she glanced over her shoulder, Zach had fallen farther behind her.

Please, God, help me get him to the hospital before it's too late.

She came to the edge of the forest. The two men were in what looked like a heated conversation as they sat in the chopper, their heads close together to be heard above the helicopter blades.

Zach came up behind her and touched her back. She could hear his raspy and uneven breathing.

"You might need this." He slipped a knife in her hand. "I have your back."

Now was the time to strike while the men were not paying attention. She darted across the open area and jumped into the back of the chopper, placing the knife against Craig's neck.

"Zach needs medical help. Take us there."

The mercenary wrinkled his forehead. "I'm not getting arrested to save your friend."

"What is going on here?" Craig blasted his question at the mercenary. "You were supposed to kill them!" The mercenary just rolled his eyes, not bothering to answer.

Zach made his way to the chopper. He walked bent over and clutching his shoulder. The mercenary looked at Craig and then at Zach. "I'll take you to the base of the mountain where you can call for help and make sure this guy goes to jail."

"You." Craig's skin turned red with rage.

Zach slumped into the seat beside Elizabeth. He reached down, grabbed some duct tape, pulled off a strip and placed it over Craig's mouth.

"Give me your hands," Zach's voice sounded weak.

Craig shook his head.

Elizabeth pressed the knife deeper into his neck. "You heard him."

Craig lifted his hands so Zach could bind them.

The helicopter lifted off while Zach secured Craig in place by duct-taping him to the chopper chair. Elizabeth dropped the knife to her side.

Zach sat back and collapsed in the seat, closing his eyes. She reached up and brushed her finger over the cheek of the man she loved and wanted to spend her life with.

She only hoped they weren't too late in getting him the medical attention he needed.

Zach awoke in the hospital bed to Elizabeth's concerned but beautiful face. She leaned in close, gripping his hand.

"How are you doing?"

"My head is really fuzzy."

"Probably all the pain meds." She squeezed his fingers.

He squeezed back. "Thanks for getting me out of there alive. You did it."

She bent closer to him and kissed his forehead. "*We* did it."

"We? The two of us together?" The look of adoration in her eyes warmed him clean through. "I meant what I said back there on the mountain. We could have a beautiful life together." He hesitated as fear gripped his heart, remembering the past rejection. "Can't we?"

Something thudded against the hospital window. Outside, Neil Thompson and another news crew had their faces pressed against the window.

"Are you kidding me?" Elizabeth bolted up and shut the shade. She laughed. "I'll be glad when this is over and we can get back to reporting the stories."

She still hadn't answered his question. "We could have a lifetime of doing that together... and of being together as man and wife," he said.

Her expression changed. She walked over to him. She leaned down and covered his lips with hers. His skin electrified at her touch. She pulled back, looking deep into his eyes. "I'd like that very much."

His heart swelled with joy, and he wrapped his arms around the woman he wanted to spend the rest of his life with. "Looks like you're stuck with me after all, Betsy," he teased.

She laughed as she squeezed his hand. "There's no place I'd rather be."

* * * * *

If you loved this story, don't miss these other exciting suspense books by Sharon Dunn

MONTANA STANDOFF
WILDERNESS TARGET
COLD CASE JUSTICE
MISTAKEN TARGET

Find more great reads at www.LoveInspired.com

Dear Reader,

I hope you enjoyed the romantic and exciting journey that Zach and Elizabeth went on. Because of his experiences being kidnapped and hounded by the press, Zach seems to have been put in Elizabeth's life when she needs a protector and someone who understands what she's going through. Both of them have been through painful and traumatic experiences. Sometimes when we are facing struggles, it is hard to understand why God might allow such pain into our lives or to believe that it might have a future purpose. During such times, it is an act of faith to trust God because He sees so much more than we can. I can say from my own life experiences that it is the painful events that have given me the opportunity to connect with other people, be empathetic and love deeply. Whatever trial you are facing today, I don't want to trivialize your pain, but I do hope you will keep your eyes on God. He is in control. Sometimes what He allows into our lives does not make sense in the present. That is when we trust in His unfailing love and focus on who He is, not on our circumstances.

Sharon Dunn

LARGER-PRINT BOOKS!

GET 2 FREE LARGER-PRINT NOVELS PLUS 2 FREE MYSTERY GIFTS

Love Inspired®

Larger-print novels are now available...

REQUEST YOUR FREE BOOKS!
2 FREE WHOLESOME ROMANCE NOVELS IN LARGER PRINT
PLUS 2
FREE
MYSTERY GIFTS

❅❅❅❅❅❅❅❅❅❅❅❅❅❅❅❅❅❅❅❅

HEARTWARMING™

❆❆❆❆❆❆❆❆❆❆❆❆❆❆❆❆❆❆❆❆

Wholesome, tender romances

YES! Please send me 2 FREE Harlequin® Heartwarming Larger-Print novels and my 2 FREE mystery gifts (gifts worth about $10). After receiving them, if I don't wish to receive any more books, I can return the shipping statement marked "cancel." If I don't cancel, I will receive 4 brand-new larger-print novels every month and be billed just $5.24 per book in the U.S. or $5.99 per book in Canada. That's a savings of at least 19% off the cover price. It's quite a bargain! Shipping and handling is just 50¢ per book in the U.S. and 75¢ per book in Canada.* I understand that accepting the 2 free books and gifts places me under no obligation to buy anything. I can always return a shipment and cancel at any time. Even if I never buy another book, the two free books and gifts are mine to keep forever.

161/361 IDN GHX2

Name _____ (PLEASE PRINT) _____

Address _____ Apt. # _____

City _____ State/Prov. _____ Zip/Postal Code _____

Signature (if under 18, a parent or guardian must sign)

Mail to the **Reader Service:**
IN U.S.A.: P.O. Box 1867, Buffalo, NY 14240-1867
IN CANADA: P.O. Box 609, Fort Erie, Ontario L2A 5X3

* Terms and prices subject to change without notice. Prices do not include applicable taxes. Sales tax applicable in N.Y. Canadian residents will be charged applicable taxes. Offer not valid in Quebec. This offer is limited to one order per household. Not valid for current subscribers to Harlequin Heartwarming larger-print books. All orders subject to credit approval. Credit or debit balances in a customer's account(s) may be offset by any other outstanding balance owed by or to the customer. Please allow 4 to 6 weeks for delivery. Offer available while quantities last.

Your Privacy—The Reader Service is committed to protecting your privacy. Our Privacy Policy is available online at www.ReaderService.com or upon request from the Reader Service.

We make a portion of our mailing list available to reputable third parties that offer products we believe may interest you. If you prefer that we not exchange your name with third parties, or if you wish to clarify or modify your communication preferences, please visit us at www.ReaderService.com/consumerchoice or write to us at Reader Service Preference Service, P.O. Box 9062, Buffalo, NY 14240-9062. Include your complete name and address.

HW15

WESTERN WP PROMISES

YES! Please send me **The Western Promises Collection** in Larger Print. This collection begins with 3 FREE books and 2 FREE gifts (gifts valued at approx. $14.00 retail) in the first shipment, along with the other first 4 books from the collection! If I do not cancel, I will receive 8 monthly shipments until I have the entire 51-book Western Promises collection. I will receive 2 or 3 FREE books in each shipment and I will pay just $4.99 US/ $5.89 CDN for each of the other four books in each shipment, plus $2.99 for shipping and handling per shipment. *If I decide to keep the entire collection, I'll have paid for only 32 books, because 19 books are FREE! I understand that accepting the 3 free books and gifts places me under no obligation to buy anything. I can always return a shipment and cancel at any time. My free books and gifts are mine to keep no matter what I decide.

272 HCN 3070 472 HCN 3070

Name _____ (PLEASE PRINT) _____

Address _____ Apt. # _____

City _____ State/Prov. _____ Zip/Postal Code _____

Signature (if under 18, a parent or guardian must sign)

Mail to the **Reader Service:**

IN U.S.A.: P.O. Box 1867, Buffalo, NY 14240-1867
IN CANADA: P.O. Box 609, Fort Erie, Ontario L2A 5X3

WPBPA16R